DATE			

Watch with Me

Other Fiction by Wendell Berry

The Discovery of Kentucky
Fidelity
The Memory of Old Jack
Nathan Coulter
A Place on Earth
Remembering
The Wild Birds

Watch with Me
And Six Other Stories
of the Yet-Remembered
Ptolemy Proudfoot
and His Wife,
Miss Minnie, Née Quinch

Wendell Berry

PANTHEON BOOKS, *New York and San Francisco*

The following stories were originally published in *The Draft Horse Journal*: "Nearly to the Fair," Autumn 1993; "Turn Back the Bed," Winter 1989; "The Lost Bet," Summer 1990; "A Consent," Autumn 1990; "A Half-Pint of Old Darling," Spring 1993; and "The Solemn Boy," 1994. "A Consent" was also published as a chapbook by Larkspur Press, Monterey, Kentucky, 1993.

Library of Congress Cataloging-in-Publication Data

Berry, Wendell, 1934–
    Watch with me : and six other stories of the yet-remembered
Ptolemy Proudfoot and his wife, Miss Minnie, née Quinch /
Wendell Berry.
        p.   cm.
      ISBN 0-679-43469-0
      1. City and town life—Kentucky—Fiction.   2. Farm life—
Kentucky—Fiction.   3. Farmers—Kentucky—Fiction.   I. Title.
PS3552.E75W3   1994
813'.54—dc20   93-48916
                                                              CIP

BOOK DESIGN BY LAURA HOUGH
Manufactured in the United States of America
FIRST EDITION
9 8 7 6 5 4 3 2 1

For Jane and Morgan Perry

Contents

Part I

Part II

For help with these stories I am grateful to Donald Hall, Don Wallis, Jack Shoemaker, Nancy Palmer Jones, and Tanya Berry.

All of these stories except for the title story first appeared in *The Draft Horse Journal*, to the editors of which I am grateful for that and for much besides. "A Consent" was published as a chapbook by my friends at Larkspur Press, Monterey, Kentucky.

Part I

1 A Consent

For my friends at Monterey

(1908)

*P*tolemy Proudfoot was nothing if not a farmer. His work was farming, his study and passion were farming, his pleasures and his social life occurred in the intervals between farm jobs and in the jobs themselves. He was not an ambitious farmer—he did not propose to own a large acreage or to become rich—but merely a good and a gifted one. By the time he was twenty-five, he had managed, in spite of the hard times of the 1890s, to make a down payment on the little farm that he husbanded and improved all his life. It was a farm of ninety-eight acres, and Tol never longed even for the two more that would have made it a hundred.

Of pleasures and social life, he had a plenty. The Proudfoots were a large, exuberant clan of large people, though by my time Tol was the last one of them in the Port William neighborhood, and Tol was childless. The Proudfoots were not, if they could help it, solitary workers. They swapped work among themselves and with their

3

neighbors, and their workdays involved a mighty dinner at noontime, much talk and laughter, and much incidental sport.

As an after-dinner amusement and aid to digestion, the Proudfoot big boys and young men would often outline a square or a circle on the ground, and get into it and wrestle. Everybody wrestled with everybody, for the object was to see who would be the last one in the ring. The manpower involved might better have been rated as horsepower, and great feats of strength were accomplished. Now and again great physical damage was accomplished, as when, for example, one Proudfoot would endeavor to throw another Proudfoot out of the ring through the trunk of a large tree. Sometimes, after failing to make headway through a tree trunk or barn door, a Proudfoot would lie very still on the ground for several minutes before he could get up. Sometimes, one Proudfoot or another would be unable to go back to work in the afternoon. These contests would be accompanied by much grunting, and by more laughter, as the Proudfoots were hard to anger. For a Proudfoot boy to become big enough and brave enough finally to set foot in that ring was a rite of passage. For a Proudfoot to stand alone in that ring—as Tol did finally, and then often did—was to know a kind of triumph and a kind of glory. Tol was big even for a Proudfoot, and the others could seldom take him off his feet. He tumbled them out, ass over elbows, one by one, in a manner more workmanly than violent, laughing all the time.

Tol was overabundant in both size and strength. And perhaps because animate creatures tended to get out of his way, he paid not much attention to himself. He damaged his clothes just by being in them, as though surprising them by an assortment of stresses and strains for which they had not been adequately prepared. The people around Port William respected Tol as a farmer; they loved to tell and retell and hear and hear again the tales of his great strength; they were amused by the looks of him, by his good humor, and by his outsized fumblings and foibles. But never, for a long time, would any of them have suspected that his great bulk might embody tender feelings.

But Tol did embody tender feelings, and very powerful tender feelings they were. For Tol, through many years, had maintained somewhere about the center of himself a most noble and humble and never-mentioned admiration for Miss Minnie Quinch. Miss Minnie was as small and quick as Tol was big and lumbering. Like him, she was a Port Williamite. She had taught for many years at Goforth School, grades one through eight, which served the neighborhood of Katy's Branch and Cotman Ridge in which Tol's farm lay. When she was hardly more than a girl, Miss Minnie had gone away to a teacher's college and prepared herself to teach by learning many cunning methods that she never afterward used. For Miss Minnie loved children and she loved books, and she taught merely by introducing the one to the other. When she had trouble with one of the rougher big boys, she went straight to that boy's father and required that measures be taken. And measures usually were taken, so surprisingly direct and demanding was that lady's gaze.

For as many years as Miss Minnie had taught at Goforth School, Tol had admired her from a distance, and without ever looking directly at her when she might have been about to look directly at him. He thought she was the finest, prettiest, nicest little woman he had ever seen. He praised her to himself by saying, "She's just a pocket-size pretty little thing." But he was sure that she would never want to be around a big, rough, unschooled fellow like himself.

Miss Minnie did, from time to time, look directly at Tol, but not ever when he might have been about to look directly at her. More than once she thought rather wistfully that so large and strong a man as Tol ought to be some woman's knight and protector. She was, in fact, somewhat concerned about him, for he was thirty-six, well past the age when men usually got married. That she herself was thirty-four and unmarried was something she also thought from time to time, but always in a different thought. She kept her concern about Tol limited very strictly to concern, for she was conscious of being a small person unable even to hope to arrest the gaze of so splendid a man.

For years, because of mutual avoidance of each other's direct gaze, their paths did not cross. Although they met and passed, they did not do so in a way that required more than a polite nod, which they both accomplished with a seriousness amounting almost to solemnity. And then one morning in Port William, Tol came out of Beater Chatham's store directly face-to-face with Miss Minnie who was coming in, and who smiled at him before she could think and said, "Well, good morning, Mr. Proudfoot!"

Tol's mouth opened, but nothing came out of it. Nothing at all. This was unusual, for Tol, when he felt like it, was a talkative man. He kept walking because he was already walking, but for several yards he got along without any assistance from his faculties. Sight and sense did not return to him until he had walked with some force into the tailgate of his wagon.

All the rest of that day he went about his work in a somewhat visionary state, saying to himself, and to the surprise of his horses and his dog, "Good morning, mam!" and "How do you do, Miss Minnie?" Once he even brought himself to say, bowing slightly and removing his hat, "And a good morning to you, little lady."

And soon, as if they had at last come into each

other's orbit, they met face-to-face again. It was a fine fall afternoon, and Tol happened to be driving down past Goforth School, slowing his team, of course, so as not to disturb the concentration of the scholars inside. Miss Minnie was standing by the pump in front of the schoolhouse, her figure making a neat blue silhouette against the dingy weatherboarding.

Again she smiled at him. She said, "How do you do, Mr. Proudfoot?"

And Tol startled at the sound of her voice as if he had not seen her there at all. He could not remember one of the pleasantries he had invented to say to her. He looked intently into the sky ahead of him and said quickly as if he had received a threat, "Why, howdy!"

The conversation thus established was a poor thing, Tol knew, so far as his own participation in it went, but it was something to go on. It gave him hope. And now I want to tell you how this courtship, conducted for so long in secret in Tol's mind alone, became public. This is the story of Miss Minnie's first consent, the beginning of their story together, which is one of the dear possessions of the history of Port William.

That fall, Miss Minnie and her students had worked hard in preparation for the annual Harvest Festival at the school. The Harvest Festival was Miss Minnie's occasion; she had thought it up herself. It might have been a Halloween party, except that Halloween in that vicinity got enough out of hand as it was without some public function to bring all the boys together in one place. And so she had thought of the Harvest Festival, which always took place two weeks before Halloween. It was a popular social event, consisting of much visiting, a display of the students' work, recitations by the students, an auction of pies and cakes to raise money for books and supplies, and abundant refreshments provided by the mothers of the students.

Ptolemy Proudfoot had never been to the Harvest Festival. He had no children, he told himself, and so did not belong there. But in fact he had always longed to go, had always been afraid to intrude himself without excuse into Miss Minnie's world, and had always, as a result, spent an unhappy night at home. But this year, now that he and Miss Minnie were in a manner of becoming friends, he determined that he would go.

Tol had got along as bachelors must. He had even become a fair cook. From the outside, his house was one of the prettiest and best kept in the neighborhood. It was a small house with steep, gingerbreaded gables, and it stood under two white oaks in the bend of the road, just before it turned down into the Katy's Branch valley where Goforth School was. Tol kept the house painted and the yard neat, and he liked to turn in off the road and say to himself, "Well, now, I wonder who lives in such a nice place!" But what he had thought up to do to the inside of the house was not a great deal above what he had thought up to do to the inside of his barn. Like the barn, the house was clean and orderly, but when he went into it, it did not seem to be expecting him, as it did after Miss Minnie came to live there.

On the day of the festival, Tol cut and shocked corn all day, but he thought all day of the festival, too, and he quit early. He did his chores, fixed his supper and ate it, and then, just as he had planned in great detail to do, he began to get ready. He brought his Sunday clothes to the kitchen and laid them out on a chair. He hunted up his Sunday shoes and polished them. He set a large washtub on the floor in front of the stove, dipped hot water into it from the water well at the end of the stove, cooled the hot water with water from the water bucket on the shelf by the door, put soap and washrag and towel on the floor beside the tub. And then he undressed and sat in the tub with his feet outside it on the floor, and scrubbed himself thoroughly from top to toe. He dried himself and put on his pants. Gazing into the mirror over the little wash table by the back door, he shaved so carefully that he cut himself in several places. He put on his shirt, and after several tries buttoned the collar. He put on his tie, tying a knot in it that would have broken the neck of a lesser man and that left even him so nearly strangled that he supposed he must look extremely handsome. He wet his hair and combed it so that when it dried it stuck up stiffly in the air as Proudfoot hair was inclined to do. He put on his suspenders, his gleaming shoes, and his Sunday hat. And then he sat in a chair and sweated and rubbed his hands together until it was time to hitch old Ike to the buggy and drive down to the school.

Before he got to the schoolhouse, he could hear voices, an uninterrupted babble like the sound of Katy's Branch in the spring, and then he could see a glow. When he got to the bottom of the hill and saw, among the trunks of the big walnuts and water maples and sycamores that stood there, the schoolhouse windows gleaming and the school yard strung with paper lanterns, lighting the bare-worn ground and throwing the shadows of the trees out in all directions like the spokes of a wheel, he said, "Whoa, Ike." The light around the old schoolhouse and within it seemed to him a radiance that emanated from the person of Miss Minnie herself. And Tol's big heart quaked within him. He had to sit there in the road behind his stopped horse and think a good while before he could decide not to go on by, pretending to have an errand elsewhere.

Now that he had stopped, it became quiet where he was; he could hear the crickets singing, and he was aware of Willow Hole on Katy's Branch, in the enclosure of trees beyond the school, carrying on its accustomed business in the dark. As he sat and thought—thought hard about nothing that he could fix in a thought—Tol slid his fingers up beneath his hat from time to time and scratched, and then jerked the hat down firmly onto his head again, and each time he did this he rotated the front of his hat a little further toward his right ear. Presently the sound of another buggy coming down the hill behind him recalled him to himself; he clucked to Ike and drove on, and found a hitching place among the other buggies and the wagons and the saddled horses at the edge of the school yard.

There was a perimeter of voices out on the very edge of the light, where the boys had started a game of tag, unwilling to come nearer the schoolhouse than they had to. Near the building the men were gathered in groups, smoking or chewing, talking, as they always talked, of crops, livestock, weather, work, prices, hunting, and fishing, in that year and the years before.

Tol, usually a sociable man, had nothing to say. He did not dare to say anything. He went past the men, merely nodding in response to their greetings, and since he did not want to talk and so could not stop, and was headed in that direction, he went on into the schoolhouse, and immediately he realized his mistake. For there were only women and girls in there, and not a single man. Beyond the boys' voices out on the edge of the dark and the men's voices in the school yard was this bright, warm nucleus of women's voices, and of women themselves and of women's eyes turned to see who had burst through the door with so much force.

Many a one of those women remembered the way Tol looked when he came in that night. After all his waiting and anxiety, his clothes were damp and wrinkled, his shirttail was out, there was horse manure on one of his shoes. His hat sat athwart his head as though left there by somebody else. When, recognizing the multiflorous female presence he was in, he snatched his hat off, his hair stuck up and out and every which way. He came in wide-eyed, purposeful, and alarmed. He looked as if only his suspenders were holding him back—as if, had it not been for that restraint upon his shoulders, he might have charged straight across the room and out through the back wall.

He had made, he thought, a serious mistake, and he was embarrassed. He was embarrassed, too, to show that he knew he had made a mistake. He did not want to stay, and he could not go. Struck dumb, his head as empty of anything sayable as a clapperless bell, he stood in one place and then another, smiling and blushing, an anxious, unhappy look in his eyes.

Finally, a voice began to speak in his mind. It was his own voice. It said, "I would give forty dollars to get out of here. I would give forty-five dollars to get out of here." It consoled him somewhat to rate his misery at so high a price. But he could see nobody to whom he could pay the forty dollars, or the forty-five either. The women had gone back to talking, and the girls to whispering.

But Tol's difficulty and his discomfort had not altogether failed of a compassionate witness. His unexpected presence had not failed to cause a small flutter in the bosom of Miss Minnie and a small change in the color of her face. As soon as she decently could, Miss Minnie excused herself from the circle of women with whom she had been talking. She took the bell from her desk and went to the door and rang it.

Presently the men and boys began to come inside. Tol, though he did not become inconspicuous, began at least to feel inconspicuous, and as his pain decreased, he was able to take intelligent notice of his whereabouts. He saw how prettily the room was done up with streamers and many candles and pictures drawn by the students and bouquets of autumn leaves and of autumn flowers. And at the head of the room on a large table were the cakes and pies that were to be auctioned off at the end of the evening. In the very center of the table, on a tall stand, was a cake that Tol knew, even before he heard, was the work of Miss Minnie. It was an angel food cake with an icing as white and light and swirly as a summer cloud. It was as white as a bride. The sight of it fairly took his breath—it was the most delicate and wondrous thing that he had ever seen. It looked so beautiful and vulnerable there all alone among the others that he wanted to defend it with his life. It was lucky, he thought, that nobody said anything bad about it—and he just wished somebody would. He took a position in a corner in the front of the room as near the cake as he dared to be, and watched over it defensively, angry at the thought of the possibility that somebody *might* say something bad about it.

"Children, please take your seats!" Miss Minnie said.

The students all dutifully sat down at their desks, leaving the grown-ups to sit or stand around the walls. There was some confusion and much shuffling of feet as everybody found a place. And then a silence, variously expectant and nervous, fell upon the room. Miss Minnie stepped to the side of her desk. She stood, her posture very correct, regarding her students and her guests in silence a moment, and then she welcomed them one and all to the annual Harvest Festival of Goforth School. She told the grown-ups how pleased she was to see them there so cherishingly gathered around their children. She gave them her heartfelt thanks for their support. She asked Brother Overhold if he would pronounce the invocation.

Brother Overhold called down the blessings of Heaven upon each and every one there assembled, and upon every family there represented; upon Goforth School and Miss Minnie, its beloved teacher; upon the neighborhood of Katy's Branch and Cotman Ridge; upon the town of Port William and all the countryside around it; upon the county, the state, the nation, the world, and the great universe, at the very center of which they were met together that night at Goforth School.

And then Miss Minnie introduced the pupils of the first grade, who were to read a story in unison. The first-grade pupils thereupon sat up straight, giving their brains the full support of their erect spinal columns, held their primers upright in front of them, and intoned loudly together:

"Once—there—were—three—*bears*. The—big—bear—was—the—*pop*pa bear. The—middle—bear—was—the—*mom*ma bear. The—little—bear—was—the—*ba*by bear"—and so on to the discovery of Goldilocks and the conclusion, which produced much applause.

And then, one by one, the older children came forward to stand at the side of the desk, as Miss Minnie had stood, to recite poems or Bible verses or bits of famous oratory.

A small boy, Billy Braymer, recited from Sir Walter Scott:

> *Breathes there the man with soul so dead*
> *Who never to himself hath said:*
> *"This is my own, my native land"?*

—and on for thirteen more lines, and said "Whew!" and sat down to enthusiastic applause. Thelma Settle of the sixth grade, one of the stars of the school, made her way through "Thanatopsis" without fault to the very end. The audience listened to "A Psalm of Life," the First, the Twenty-third, and the Hundredth Psalms, "The Fool's Prayer," "To a Waterfowl," "To Daffodils," "Concord Hymn," "The Choir Invisible," "Wolsey's Farewell to His Greatness," Hamlet's Soliloquy, "The Epitaph" from Gray's "Elegy Written in a Country Church-Yard," and other pieces. Hibernia Hopple of the eighth grade declared with a steadily deepening blush and in furious haste that she loved to the depth and breadth and height her soul could reach. Walter Crow said in a squeaky voice and with bold gestures that he was the master of his fate and the captain of his soul. Buster Niblett implored that he be given liberty or death.

And then Miss Minnie called the name of Burley Coulter, and a large boy stood up in the back of the room and, blushing, made his way to the desk as he would have walked, perhaps, to the gallows. He turned and faced the audience. He shut his eyes tightly, opened them only to find the audience still present, and swallowed. Miss Minnie watched him with her fingers laced at her throat and her eyes moist. He was such a good-looking boy, and—she had no doubt—was smart. Against over-powering evidence she had imagined a triumph for him. She had chosen a poem for him that was masculine, robust, locally applicable, seasonally appropriate, high-spirited, and amusing. If he recited it well, she would be so pleased! She had the poem in front of her, just in case.

He stood in silence, as if studying to be as little present as possible, and then announced in an almost inaudible voice, " 'When the Frost Is on the Punkin' by James Whitcomb Riley."

He hung his hands at his sides, and then clasped them behind him, and then clasped them in front of him, and then put them into his pockets. He swallowed a dry-mouthed swallow that in the silence was clearly audible, and began:

> *"When the frost is on the punkin and the fodder's in the shock,*
> *And you hear the kyouck and gobble of the struttin' turkey-cock,*
> *And the clackin' of the—of the,* uh—*the clackin' of the—"*

"Guineys!" Miss Minnie whispered.

"Aw, yeah, guineys," he said:

> *"And the clackin' of the guineys, and the cluckin' of the hens,*
> *And the rooster's hallylooyer as he tiptoes on the fence—*
> uh, let's see—"

"Oh, it's then's . . ."

> *"Oh, it's then's the time's a feller is a-feelin' at his best,*
> *With the risin' sun to greet him from a night of peaceful rest,*
> *When he—*uh—"

"As he leaves . . ."

> *"As he leaves the house, bare-headed, and goes out to feed the stock,*
> *When the frost is on the punkin and the fodder's in the shock."*

He looked at his feet, he scratched his head, his lips moved soundlessly.

"They's something . . ."

"Aw, yeah.

"They's something kindo' harty-like about the atmusfere
When the heat of summer's over—uh—*kindo' lonesome-*
like, but still—uh—

"Well, let's see. Uh—

"Then your apples—Then your apples all—"

Miss Minnie was reading desperately, trying to piece the poem together as he dismembered it, but he had left her behind and now he was stalled. She looked up to see an expression on his face that she knew too well. The blush was gone; he was grinning; the light of inspiration was in his eyes.

"Well, drot it, folks," he said, "I forgot her. But I'll tell you one I *heard*."

Miss Minnie rose, smiling, and said in a tone of utter gratification, *"Thank* you, Burley! Now you may be seated."

She then called upon Kate Helen Branch, who came to the front and sang "In the Gloaming" in a voice that was not strong but was clear and true.

That brought the recitations to an appropriate conclusion. There was prolonged applause, after which Miss

Minnie again arose. "Mr. Willis Bagby," she said, "will now conduct our auction of pies and cakes."

Mr. Bagby took his place behind the table of pies and cakes.

"Folks," he said, "this here is for the good of the school, and to help out this little teacher here that's doing such a good job a-teaching our children. For what would tomorrow be without the young people of today? And what would our young people be without a fine teacher to teach them to figger and read and write, and to make them do all the fine things we seen them do here on this fine occasion this evening? So now, folks, open up your hearts and let out your pocketbooks. What am I bid for this fine cherry pie?" And he tilted the pie toward the crowd so that all could see the lovely crisscrossing of the top crust.

Tol had stood and watched and listened in a state of anxiety that prevented him from benefiting at all from the program. He had never seen in his life, he thought, such a woman as Miss Minnie—she was so smart and pretty, and so knowing in how to stand and speak. And when she stopped that Burley Coulter and set him down, Tol felt his heart swerve like a flying swift. She was as quick on her feet, he thought, as a good hind-catcher. And yet the more he looked upon her, the higher above him she shone, and the farther he felt beneath her notice.

Now there was old Willis Bagby auctioning off the pies and cakes, which were bringing more or less than fifty cents, depending on what they looked like and who had made them. And Tol was sweating and quaking like a man afraid. For what if *her* cake brought *less* than fifty cents? What if—and he felt his heart swerve again—nobody bid on it? He would bid on it himself—but how could he dare to? People would think he was trying to show off. Maybe *she* would think he was trying to show off.

Tol backed into his corner as far as he could, trying to be small, wishing he had not come. But now Willis Bagby put his hands under the beautiful white cake and lifted it gleaming on its stand.

"*Now* look a-here, folks," he said. "For last, we got this fine cake made by this mighty nice lady, our school-teacher. What am I bid for it?"

"One dollar," said Gilead Hopple, who with his wife, Ag, was standing not far in front of Tol Proudfoot. Gil Hopple was the local magistrate, who now proposed for himself the political gallantry of offering the highest bid for the teacher's cake. After his bid, he uttered a small cough.

"Dollar bid! I've got a dollar bid," said Willis Bagby. "Now, anywhere a half?"

Nobody said anything. Nobody said anything for a time that got longer and longer, while Gil Hopple stood there with his ears sticking out and his white bald head sticking up through its official fringe of red hair.

And Tol Proudfoot was astonished to hear himself

say right out and in a voice far too loud, *"Two dollars!"*

Gil Hopple coughed his small cough again and said, his voice slightly higher in pitch than before, "Two and a quarter."

It seemed to Tol that Gil Hopple had defiled that priceless cake with his quarter bid. Gil Hopple happened to be Tol's neighbor, and they had always got along and been friends. But at that moment Tol hated Gil Hopple with a clean, clear, joyful hatred. He said, *"Three* dollars!"

Gil Hopple did not wish to turn all the way around, but he looked first to the right and then to the left. His ears stuck out farther, and the top of his head had turned pink. It had been a dry year. He looked as if the room smelled of an insufficient respect for hard cash. "Three and a quarter," he said in a tone of great weariness.

Willis Bagby was looking uncomfortable himself now. Things obviously were getting out of hand, but it was not up to him to stop it.

Tol said, "Four!"

At that point a revelation came to Miss Minnie. It seemed to her beyond a doubt that Tol Proudfoot, that large, strong man whom she had thought ought to be some woman's knight and protector, was bidding to be *her* knight and protector. It made her dizzy. She managed to keep her composure: she did not blush much, the tears hardly showed in her eyes, by great effort she did not breathe much too fast. But her heart was staggering within her like a drunk person, and she was saying over and over to herself, "Oh, you magnificent man!"

"Four and a quarter," said Gil Hopple.

"*Five!*" said Tol Proudfoot.

"Five and a quarter," said Gil Hopple.

"*Ten!*" shouted Tol Proudfoot.

And at that moment another voice—Ag Hopple's—was raised above the murmuring of the crowd: "Good *lord*, Gil! I'll *make* you a cake!"

Willis Bagby, gratefully seeing his duty, said, "Sold! To Tol Proudfoot yonder in the corner."

Tol could no more move than if he had been turned by his audacity into a statue. He stood in his corner with sweat running down his face, unable to lift his hand to wipe it off, frightened to think how he had showed off right there in front of everybody for her to see.

And then he saw that Miss Minnie was coming to where he was, and his knees shook. She was coming through the crowd, looking straight at him, and smiling. She reached out with her little hand and put it into one of his great ones, which rose of its own accord to receive it. "Mr. Proudfoot," she said, "that was more than kind."

Tol was standing there full in public view, in the midst of a story that Port William would never forget, and as far as he now knew not a soul was present but Miss Minnie and himself.

"Yes, mam—uh, mam—uh, miss—uh, little

lady," he said. "Excuse me, mam, but I believe it was worth every cent of it, if you don't mind. And I ain't trying to act smart or anything, and if I do, excuse me, but might I see you home?"

"Oh, Mr. Proudfoot!" Miss Minnie said. "Certainly you may!"

2 A Half-Pint of
Old Darling

(1920)

Ptolemy Proudfoot and Miss Minnie did not often take a lively interest in politics. They were Democrats, like virtually everybody else in the vicinity of Cotman Ridge and Goforth. They had been born Democrats, had never been anything but Democrats, and had never thought of being anything but Democrats. To them, being Democrats was much the same sort of thing as being vertebrates; it was not a matter of lively interest. Their daily lives were full of matters that were in the most literal sense lively: gardens and crops and livestock, kitchen and smokehouse and cellar, shed and barn and pen, plantings and births and harvests, washing and ironing and cooking and canning and cleaning, feeding and milking, patching and mending. That their life was surrounded by great public issues they knew and considered, and yet found a little strange.

The year 1920, however, was one of unusually lively political interest, especially for Miss Minnie. In January of that year, the constitutional amendment forbidding "the manufacture, sale, or transportation of intoxicating liquors" went into effect. And in August the women's suffrage amendment was ratified. Miss Minnie did not approve of drinking intoxicating liquors, which she believed often led to habitual drunkenness. And she certainly did believe that women ought to have the vote.

Tol, for his part, enjoyed a bottle of beer occasionally, and occasionally he had been known to enjoy a good drink of somebody else's whiskey—whether homemade or bottled in bond he did not particularly care, so long as it was good. He liked whiskey of a quality to cure a sore throat, not cause one. This was not something that Miss Minnie knew or that Tol had ever considered telling her. It was not something she had ever had any occasion—or, so far as he knew, any need—to know. Liquor also was something that he could easily go without. If the country chose not to drink, then he could comfortably endure the deprivation as long as the country could.

And so very little was said between them on the subject of the Prohibition amendment. Miss Minnie belonged to the Women's Christian Temperance Union, and supported the amendment, and that was all right with Tol, and that was that.

On the question of the suffrage amendment, Tol's conclusion was that if he had the vote, and if (as he believed) Miss Minnie was smarter than he was, then

Miss Minnie should have the vote. Miss Minnie (who did not think she was smarter than Tol, and did not wish to be) said that though Tol had not accurately weighed all the evidence, his reasoning was perfect.

"The vote," said Tol, "means that us onlookers and bystanders get to have a little bit of say-so."

"And I want my little bit," Miss Minnie said.

"So it's out with the whiskey and in with the women," Tol said.

Miss Minnie let him have a smile then, for she loved his wit, but she said that by and large she thought that was the way it would have to be, for women hated liquor because of all they'd had to suffer from drunken men. She had seen some of her own students grow up to be worthless drunkards.

Tol said that she was right there, and he knew it. By and large, he was content to believe as she believed. She had been a schoolteacher and knew books, and he looked up to her.

To say that Tol looked up to Miss Minnie is to use a figure of speech, for Tol was an unusually big man and Miss Minnie an unusually small woman. And so at the moment when he was in spirit looking up to her, he was in the flesh beaming down upon her from beneath a swatch of hair that projected above his brows like a porch roof.

A Half-Pint of Old Darling

It was still dark on a morning in early November. Tol had done his chores while Miss Minnie fixed breakfast; they had eaten and, having completed their conversation, had stood up from the table. Tol's hair, which he had wetted and combed when he washed his face, had reverted to its habit of sticking out this way and that. This condition had been aggravated by Tol's habit of scratching under his cap from time to time without taking it off. To an impartial observer Tol might have looked a little funny, as though he had put a pile of jackstraws on his head.

Miss Minnie, however, was not an impartial observer. To her he looked comfortable. To her he was shelter and warmth. When he smiled down at her that way, it was to her as though the sun itself had looked kindly at her through the foliage of a tall tree.

It was a Saturday morning. That day they were going to make one of their twice- or thrice-yearly trips to Hargrave, the county seat, ten miles down the river from Port William, nearly fourteen miles from their house. They had lists of things they needed to do or buy that they could not do or buy at the store at Goforth or at Port William. And each of them had a little bit of secret Christmas shopping to do.

Tol said he had a few odds and ends to do at the barn before he harnessed Redbird. And Miss Minnie said that would be fine, for she had to finish up in the house and ought to be ready by the time he would be.

Tol said, well, he thought they needn't to be in a big hurry, for it was a little nippy out, and maybe they should give it a chance to warm up. And Miss Minnie said, yes, that was fine.

And so in the slowly strengthening gray November daylight Tol set things to rights around the barn, the way he liked to do on Saturday, and brought Redbird out of his stall and curried and brushed and harnessed him, and left him hitched in the driveway of the barn. Tol pulled the buggy out of its shed then and went back to the house. He shaved at the washstand by the kitchen door and put on the fresh clothes that Miss Minnie had laid out for him.

Miss Minnie had the gift of neatness. Her house was neat, and she was neat herself. Even in her everyday dresses she always looked as if she were expecting company. This, in addition to her fineness of mind and character, made her, Tol thought, a person of quality. Tol loved the word *quality* much as he loved the words of horse anatomy such as *pastern*, *stifle*, and *hock*. He liked it when a buyer said to him of his crop or a load of lambs or steers, "Well, Mr. Proudfoot, I see you've come with quality again this year." And when he thought about what a fine woman Miss Minnie was, with her neat ways and her book learning and her correct grammar, he enjoyed saying to himself, "She's got quality."

Tol was like Miss Minnie in his love of neatness, and his farm was neatly kept. His barn was as neat in its way as Miss Minnie's house. But Tol was not a neat person. He was both too big, I assume, and too forgetful of himself to look neat in his clothes. The only time Tol's clothes looked good was before he put them on. In putting them on, he forgot about them and began, without the slightest malice toward them, to subject them to various forms of abuse. When he had got them on that morning, Miss Minnie came in and went over them, straightening his shirtfront, buttoning his cuffs, tucking in his pocket handkerchief and the end of his belt. She pecked over his clothes with concentrated haste, like a banty hen pecking over a barn floor, as if Tol were not occupying them at all, Tol meanwhile ignoring her as he transferred his pocket stuff from his discarded pants and put on his cap and coat.

"Now you look all nice," she said.

And Tol said, "You look mighty nice, too, little lady." That was his endearment, and she gave him a pat.

The sun had come up behind clouds, and from the looks of the sky it would be cloudy all day.

"Is it going to rain?" Miss Minnie said.

"I doubt it," Tol said. "May snow along about evening, from the looks of things and the feel of that wind."

They went together to where the buggy stood. Tol brought Redbird from the barn and put him between the shafts, handed Miss Minnie up into the buggy, and got in himself, the buggy tilting somewhat to his side as his weight bore on the springs, so that it was natural for Miss Minnie to sit close to him. Sitting close to him was not something she ever minded, but on that morning it was particularly gratifying, for the wind, as Tol said, was "a little blue around the edges." They snugged the lap robe around them and drove out onto the road.

For a while they did not talk. Redbird was a young horse in those days, Tol having hitched him for the first time only that spring, and he was feeling good. The sharp air made him edgy. He was startled by the steam clouds of his breath, and he enjoyed the notion that he was in danger of being run over by the buggy rolling behind him.

"Cutting up like a new pair of scissors, ain't he?" Tol said. "Whoa, my little Redbird! Whoa, my boy! Settle down, now!" Tol sang to the colt in a low, soothing voice. "You'll be thinking different thoughts by dark."

Redbird and his notions amused Tol. He gave him his head a little, letting him trot at some speed.

"He requires a steady hand, doesn't he?" Miss Minnie said, impressed as always by Tol's horsemanship.

"He's a little notional," Tol said. "He'll get over it."

Redbird abandoned his notions about halfway up the first long hill, and settled down to a steady jog. Tol could relax then, and he and Miss Minnie resumed their never-ending conversation about the things they saw along the road and the things those sights reminded them of, and this morning, too, they talked more from time to time about politics.

What brought the subject up now, as at breakfast, was that in this year of unusual political interest Latham Gallagher was running for the office of state represen- tative. "The Gallagher boy," as Miss Minnie called him, had been sheriff and court clerk, and now he aspired to the seat of government in Frankfort. He was the son of an old friend of Miss Minnie's, and for that reason Miss Minnie thought him fine and handsome and an excellent orator. A month or so ago she and Tol had gone to hear him speak on the porch of the old hotel in Port William.

Tol thought that the Gallagher boy had already made far too much of some of his opportunities, and he did not like oratory made up of too many sentences be- ginning "My fellow Kentuckians," but he kept his opin- ions to himself. The boy, after all, was a Democrat, which meant that there was at least one worse thing he could have been.

Now and again as they drove along, Tol and Miss Minnie would see one of the Gallagher boy's posters attached to a tree or a telephone pole. "Gallagher for Representative," the posters said, "A Fair Shake for the Little Man."

"A Fair Shake for the Little Woman," said Tol

Proudfoot, nudging Miss Minnie beneath the lap robe, and she nudged him back.

They went through Port William and on down the river road to Ellville and over the bridge into Hargrave, talking the whole way. It had been a busy fall; Tol had been out of the house from daylight to dark, and Miss Minnie had been equally preoccupied with her own work, preparing for winter. So it was pleasant to ride along behind the now-dutiful Redbird, in no particular hurry, and just visit, telling each other all they'd thought of and meant to say as soon as they found a chance.

When they got to Hargrave, they left Redbird at the livery stable where he could rest well and have some hay to eat and a ration of grain while they went about their errands. At first they did a little shopping together, and carried their purchases back and stored them in the buggy. And then they went to the Broadfields Hotel to eat dinner. This was a place Tol particularly favored because they did not bring the meals out on individual plates to little separate tables, but instead the patrons sat together at long tables, and the food was set before them on heaped platters and in large bowls, and pans of hot biscuits and cornbread were passing around almost continuously, and pitchers of sweet milk and buttermilk and pots of coffee were always in reach, and when a person's plate began to look clean, there would be waiters coming around with various kinds of pie, and all of it was good. It was a place where a man like Tol could eat all he wanted without calling too much attention to himself—cooking for him, Miss Minnie had been heard to say, was like cooking for a hotel—and where also he could have his fill of conversation. Tol loved to eat and he loved to talk. The hotel dining room appealed to him because while he ate there he could expect to be in the company of some people he knew and of some he did not know, and in the course of a meal he would extract from all of them a great deal of information about themselves, their families, and their businesses or farms—also their opinions about the national and local economies, the market prospects for tobacco, cattle, sheep, and hogs, and any other opinions they might care to express. The meal characteristically would take an hour and a half or two hours, for Tol stretched to the limit the leisure and the pleasure of it. It was one of the main reasons for their trip to Hargrave, as Miss Minnie knew, though Tol never said so. He ate and talked and laughed and complimented the cooks and urged more food on his fellow guests just as if he were at home.

When the meal was over and they had lingered, talking, at the table for long enough, Tol and Miss Minnie strolled out onto the hotel porch, from which they could see the broad Ohio River flowing past and the mouth of their own smaller river opening into it. The ferry that connected Hargrave with the nearby towns in Indiana pulled away from the dock while they watched.

And then Miss Minnie, who wanted to buy Tol's Christmas present, a little awkwardly presented the falsehood that she had "a few little errands" and would meet him at the livery stable in an hour and a half. Her business would not require that long, but she knew that Tol, wherever he went, would get to talking and would be that long at least. Tol, who wished to do some private shopping of his own, agreed, and they parted.

Tol first returned to a dry goods store that he and Miss Minnie had visited together that morning. He had heard her say to a clerk of a certain bolt of cloth, intending perhaps that he should overhear, "Now *that's* pretty." He bought her enough of the cloth to make a dress. And then, because it took so little cloth to make a dress for Miss Minnie, he went to another store and bought her a pretty comb that caught his eye, and also—what he had never done before—a bottle of perfume, which lasted for years and years because, as Miss Minnie said, it smelled so wonderful that she used it seldom and only the teensiest bit at a time. He stuck these things into various pockets to be smuggled home, talked with the clerk until another customer came in, and went back out to the street.

*T*he thought struck him then that he might not get back to Hargrave before his ewes started to lamb, and he was out of whiskey. Tol always liked to keep a little whiskey on hand during lambing. Some sheepmen would say that if you had a weak lamb and a bottle of whiskey, it paid better to knock the lamb in the head and drink the whiskey yourself. But Tol believed that "a drop or two," on a bitter night, would sometimes encourage a little heart to continue beating—as, despite his religion and Miss Minnie, he believed it had sometimes encouraged bigger ones to do.

And so, without giving the matter much thought, he went to the drugstore where he was used to buying the occasional half-pint that he needed. And then, as he entered the door, he thought, "Prohibition!" And then he thought, "Well, no harm in trying."

So he went up to the druggist, whom he knew, who was leaning against a wall of shelves behind the counter in the back.

"I don't reckon you could let me have half a pint of whiskey," Tol said to him in a low voice.

"Medicinal?" the druggist asked.

"Medicinal," Tol said, nodding.

The druggist handed him a half-pint bottle, and Tol stuck it into his pocket and paid. It was a local brand known as Old Darling—a leftover, Tol supposed.

The druggist, also a conversationalist, said, "Somebody a little under the weather?"

"No," Tol said. "Lambs. I like to have a little on hand when I'm lambing."

There followed an exchange of some length in which Tol and the druggist told each other a number of things that both of them already knew.

When he was back at the livery stable, hitching Redbird to the buggy, Tol remembered the bottle and tossed it onto the floor of the buggy box under the seat, thinking not much about it one way or another.

Redbird, well rested and fed and now going in his favorite direction, required a good bit of attention at first. They were across the bridge and well out into the country again before he settled down. When he settled down, Tol settled down, too, and so did Miss Minnie. The interests and pleasures of the town were all behind them, the trip had fulfilled its purposes, and now they had ahead of them only the long drive home and their evening chores, which would seem a little strange after their day in town. Tol drove with his eye on Redbird and the road ahead, humming to himself in a grunty, tuneless way that meant, Miss Minnie knew, that he had gone way off among his thoughts and no longer knew she was there. "Mr. Proudfoot," she had actually said to him once, "when you are thinking you might as well be asleep."

That made him laugh, for he enjoyed a good joke on himself. But it was true. Sometimes, in his thoughts, he departed from where he was.

———

Tol and Miss Minnie had been married for twelve years. In that time they had found how secret their lives had been before. They had made many small discoveries that were sometimes exciting, sometimes not. One of the best had been Tol's discovery that Miss Minnie could whistle.

Though he had known a whistling woman or two in his time, he had always known also the proverb holding that

> These will come to no good end:
> A whistling woman and a crowing hen,

and he assumed that Miss Minnie, who had quality, would be the last woman on earth to whistle. Imagine his surprise, then, not long after they were married, when he was going by the house one morning and overheard Miss Minnie rattling the breakfast dishes and whistling "Old Joe Clark" as prettily and effortlessly as a songbird.

That night after supper, when they were sitting together by the fire, he said to her, "Go ahead. Whistle. I know you can do it. I heard you."

So she whistled for him—"Soldier's Joy" this time. It was a secret revelation. It made them so gleeful she could hardly control her pucker.

And now I am going to tell about the more famous revelation by which Miss Minnie learned Tol's method of reviving a weak lamb.

Tol had been humming and thinking only a little while when Miss Minnie needed to blow her nose. Her handkerchief was in her purse, which she had set behind her heels under the seat of the buggy. She fished under the lap robe with her hand to bring it up and so encountered the cold hard shape of Tol's half-pint bottle of Old Darling. It was a shape that, as an avid student of the problem of drunkenness, she knew very well. Thereupon a suspicion flew into her mind—as sudden and dark as a bat this suspicion was, and as hard to ignore in such close quarters.

She felt the bottle again to make sure, and then stealthily drew it up to the light on the side opposite Tol, and looked at it. At the sight of it, she could have wept and cried out with anger and with bitter, bitter disappointment. The label carried the seductive name of Old Darling, and it declared shamelessly that the bottle contained whiskey, ninety proof. That the amber liquid inside the bottle was actually rather beautiful to the eye did not surprise her, for she knew that the devil made sin attractive.

She almost flung the bottle into the roadside weeds right there and then, but two thoughts prevented her. First, she imagined that if the bottle did not hit a rock and break, then some innocent boy or young man might come along and find it and be tempted to drink the whiskey, and that would not do. Second—and perhaps this thought was not even second, for her mind was working fast—she remembered that whiskey was an expensive product. When she thought, "It would be a shame to waste it," she meant of course the money that Tol had spent for the whiskey, not the whiskey itself.

But she did think, "It would be a shame to waste it," and the thought put her in a quandary. For if she did not want to throw the whiskey away, neither did she want to put it back under the seat to be carried home and drunk by her wayward husband, from the mystery of whose being this bottle had emerged.

And now Miss Minnie's mind revolved in a curious metamorphosis from the great virtue of thriftiness to the much smaller virtue of romantic self-sacrifice. Her anger and disappointment at Tol as she now had discovered him to be only increased her love for him as she had thought him to be—and as he might, in fact, become, if only she could save him from his addiction to the evil drug that she at that moment held in her hand. For such a man as he *might* be, she felt, she would do anything. She had read much of loyalties given and sacrifices made by the wives of drinking men. In her love for Tol, she had at times already wished to be capable of some legendary fidelity or sacrifice to make her worthy of her happiness in him. And by how much now was this wish magnified by her thought of Tol fallen and redeemed! "Oh," she thought, "I will do it! I will say to the world I did it without hesitation." She shifted as she might have shifted if she had wanted to look at something interesting off to the right-hand side of the road.

She broke the paper seal and twisted out the cork. She put her nose carefully over the opening and sniffed the vile fumes. *"Awful!"* she thought. And the thought of its awfulness made her sacrifice more pleasing to her. She tilted the bottle and drew forth bravely half a mouthful and swallowed it.

It was fire itself in her throat. If she had looked quickly enough, she thought, she would have seen a short orange flame protruding from her nose. Though she sternly suppressed the impulse to cough, there was no refusing the tears that filled her eyes.

But then as the fiery swallow descended into her stomach, a most pleasing warmth, a warmth at once calming and invigorating, began to radiate from it. For a few minutes she bestowed upon this warmth the meditation that it seemed to require, and then she tried another swallow, a more wholehearted one. The effect this time was less harsh, because less surprising, and the radiance even warmer and more reassuring than before. She felt strangely ennobled by the third, as if the rewards of her sacrifice were already accruing to her. The radiance within her had begun to gleam also in a sort of nimbus around her. If the devil made sin attractive, then she would have to admit that he had done a splendid job with Old Darling.

She sat half turned away from Tol, and leaning back so that she sat also a little behind him. He was still departed in his thoughts, no more aware of what she was doing than were the occupants of the occasional buggies and wagons that they met.

Miss Minnie sipped from time to time as they drove along, finding her sacrifice not nearly so difficult as she had expected. In fact, she was amazed at how quickly she was getting rid of the repulsive contents of the bottle. It occurred to her that perhaps she should drink more slowly, for soon there would be none left.

Suddenly she experienced a motion that recalled her to her school days when she had swung in swings and ridden on seesaws. But the likeness was only approximate, for Redbird, the buggy, the road, and indeed the whole landscape had just executed a motion not quite like any she had ever known.

"Whoo!" said Miss Minnie.

Tol had been humming along, figuring and re-figuring how much he might get for his crop in view of the various speculations and surmises he had heard in town. When Miss Minnie said "Whoo!" it was news to him. "What?" he said.

"Do that again," she said. "Oh! Whoo!"

He said, "What?"

"Old Darling," she said. "Whoo!"

"Mam?" Tol Proudfoot said.

And then he saw the bottle in her hand. For a moment he thought he was going to laugh, and then he thought he wasn't. "Oh, Lordy!" he said. "Oh, Lordy Lord! Oh, Lord!"

Now as they went around a curve in the road they met another couple in a buggy. Miss Minnie leaned forward and called out to them momentously the name of Gallagher. "A vote for Gallagher," she cried, "is a vote for the little man!"

"Come up, Redbird," said Tol Proudfoot.

But as luck would have it, speeding up only brought them more quickly face to face with the next buggy coming down the road.

"Gallagher!" cried Miss Minnie. "A fair shake for the little man is a fair shake for the little woman!"

"Miss Minnie," Tol said, "I believe you've had about all you need of that."

He held out his hand for the bottle, and was surprised to see, when she handed it to him, how little was left.

"Take it, then!" she said. "Drunkard!"

"Drunkard?" he said, and then put out his hand again to steady her, for she was attempting to stand up, the better to point her finger at him. "No, mam. I'm not no drunkard. You know better."

"Then *what*," Miss Minnie said, pointing to the incontrovertible evidence, "were you doing with *that*?"

"Lambs," Tol said.

"You get little lambs drunk," Miss Minnie declared. "Oh, my dear man, you *are* the limit."

"For when they're born on the cold nights," Tol said. "Sometimes it'll help the weak ones live."

"Ha!" said Miss Minnie.

Tol said no more. Miss Minnie spoke only to urge Gallagher upon the people they met—though, fortunately, they met only a few.

By the time they went through Port William, she had ceased to call out, but she was saying in a rather loud voice and to nobody in particular that though she was not sure, she was sure the Gallagher boy had never taken a drink in *his* life—and though she was not sure, she was sure that *he* at least understood that now that women had the vote, there would be no more liquor drinking in the land of the free and the home of the brave. Her voice quivered patriotically.

When they drove in beside the house at last, and Redbird gladly stopped in front of the buggy shed, Tol stepped down and turned to help Miss Minnie, who stood, somewhat grandly spurning his offer, and fell directly into his arms.

Tol carried her to the house, helped her to remove her hat and coat and to lie down on the sofa in the living room. He covered her with the afghan, built up the fire, and returned to the barn to do his chores.

The house was dark when he came back in. Miss Minnie was lying quietly on the sofa with her forearm resting across her brow. Tol tiptoed in and sat down.

After a little while, Miss Minnie said, "Was it really just for the lambs?"

Tol said, "Yessum."

And then Miss Minnie's crying jag began. Regrets flew at her from all sides, and she wept and wept. Of all her sorrows the worst was for her suspicion of Tol. But she mourned also, for his sake and her own, the public display that she had made of herself. "I surely am the degradedest woman who ever lived," she said. "I have shamed myself, and most of all you."

Tol sat beside her for a long time in the dark, patting her with his big hand and saying, "Naw, now. Naw, now. You didn't do no such of a thing."

It was, as Miss Minnie would later say, a lovely time.

When at last she grew quiet and sleepy, Tol helped her to bed and waited beside her until her breath came in little snores. And then he went down to the kitchen and cooked himself a good big supper, for it had been a hard day.

———

*T*his was, oddly, a tale that Miss Minnie enjoyed telling. "It was my only binge," she would say, giggling a little. And she liked especially to quote herself: "I surely am the degradedest woman who ever lived."

She said, "Mr. Proudfoot was horrified. But after it was over, he just had to rear back and laugh. Oh, he was a man of splendid qualities!"

3 The Lost Bet

(1929)

*A*fter Ptolemy Proudfoot and Miss Minnie bought their Model A and partly quit using their buggy, they got around in the neighborhood more than they used to. But only a little more. Tol was never the master of the Model A that he was of a horse; if the car increased by a little bit the frequency of their going about, it increased their range almost not at all—except once, which is another story. For Tol and Miss Minnie, the Model A was an experiment—the only one they ever made—and it did not completely replace their horse and buggy, which Tol kept and continued to use for shorter trips until his death. He *liked* horses better than he liked the Model A, and he drove them better, too.

Before and after the advent of the Model A, Tol and Miss Minnie lived their lives almost entirely within a radius of about four miles. They cleaned up after dinner every Saturday and drove the four miles to Port William to take their cream and eggs, and to buy the few things they needed that they did not grow or make for themselves. All their business never took more than an hour, but they made an afternoon of it, visiting and talking with everybody else who had come in for the same purposes, and always getting back home in plenty of time to milk and feed.

On Sunday morning they went a mile in the other direction to the Goforth church, usually going back again for the evening services. And once a month Miss Minnie attended the all-day meeting of the Missionary Society. And that was most of their going, except when they went to a wedding or a funeral or to a neighbor's house to visit or help with the work.

And except for an occasional trip, which Tol sometimes made alone, to Hargrave or to the stockyards in Louisville. He sold his tobacco at Hargrave, where there was also a small stockyard. But Tol was a pretty shrewd businessman, and when he had enough stock to justify the haulage—as when he shipped his lambs in June, and his finished steers in November—he liked to try the market at the Bourbon Stockyards in Louisville. The prices were noticeably better there than at Hargrave, but that was not all the reason. The rest of it was that Tol enjoyed making the trip with Sam Hanks, the trucker who hauled the stock. And Sam Hanks found it necessary to admit that he enjoyed making the trip with Tol. Sam Hanks was Miss Minnie's favorite nephew, a lean, seldom-speaking man, who might go all day and not speak ten words, just doing his work and watching and being amused. He was a little amused at whatever happened—at least in his younger days. His major amusements were baseball and Tol. Over the years he collected a lot of stories about Tol, and he liked to tell them.

Tol would be up long before daylight on the appointed day, getting the steers or the lambs penned and ready to load. And then he would feed and milk and eat breakfast and clean up, so as to be ready when, maybe still before daylight, Sam's truck would rattle up the driveway past the house into the barn lot, and back up to the loading chute.

Tol was a fellow who was neat as a pin in all his work, but who was to about the same degree careless of his own appearance. His little farm was almost as clean and orderly as Miss Minnie's kitchen, which was immaculate. When he drove his team to the field they were as well groomed and harnessed as if he were driving them to town. And he used a plow or a mowing machine as precisely as some people use a comb. But he wore his clothes, as Sam Hanks said, the way a hog wears mud.

When he left the house to load his stock, he would be as clean and neat as Miss Minnie's repeated instructions and inspections could make him. He would be washed and shaved and combed, dressed in his best everyday clothes, which would be spotless, as stiff with starch as if made of tin. By the time the stock were loaded, all

49

the creases would be crisscrossed with wrinkles; there would be mud and manure on his shoes and britches and maybe on his shirt; he would have a loose cuff or suspender; after much head scratching, his cap or hat would be on crooked and some stray swatch of hair would be hanging in his eyes or sticking out over one ear.

After they got to the stockyards and got unloaded, Tol followed a procedure that in its general outlines never varied. And Sam always went along in a state of alert expectancy, because in its details it was never twice the same. Say it was in the fall. They would go back through the yards to where Tol's steers were penned, and lean against the gate to wait for the buyers to come around. But it wasn't just the buyers, Sam knew, that Tol was waiting for. Tol always had good steers—good in their individual quality, uniform as a lot, and well finished, showing a lot of bloom—and he liked to hear them praised. And so he stood there, leaning proprietarily against the gate, watching the drovers and the commission men and the farmers go by. And when one of them stopped to look into the pen at Tol's cattle, Tol would look at him in such a way that the fellow nearly always asked, "Those your steers?"

And Tol would say, "*Ye*ssir!" as if it ought to have been obvious.

And then the fellow would say something like "Mighty nice" or "Well, they're the right kind."

And Tol would say, "*Ye*ssir!" in a way that showed

he knew the fellow had made pretty much of an understatement—which sometimes caused the fellow to try to say something even better and more intelligent about the cattle, and sometimes did not.

If it did not, Tol would turn the conversation to the subject of the fellow himself—what his name was, where he was from, whom he had married, how his family was, how much rain he'd had, how his crops had turned off, and so on. Tol loved that kind of visiting, and he talked to everybody he met whether the body in question wanted to be talked to or not. Sam followed these conversations with as much interest as he followed baseball. The thing was that Tol mostly liked everybody, and because he liked them he was genuinely interested in everything about them, and he pumped information out of them, Sam figured, that would be news to their wives. Tol never forgot them or anything he learned about them, and he was always glad to see them when he met them again. He had got acquainted with a lot of people in this way. But Sam knew that on these trips, because they were his adventures, Tol much preferred strangers to acquaintances.

When the cattle were sold and the talking was finished, they went to the office for their checks. Except for the few times when Tol thought his stock had been graded too low, Sam never heard him complain about the size of his check. He appeared to accept it simply as the necessary completion of a business in which he had ceased to have any live interest the moment the cattle ceased to belong to him.

And then Tol would invite Sam to be his guest at a certain poolroom where, if it was fall, they would eat fried oysters, which Tol loved. The meal lasted an hour or two. They stood at the bar and ate, and Tol talked to whatever stranger happened to be standing next to him. Now, for Sam, the quality of the interest changed, for here Tol was less likely to be talking to a farmer and more likely to be talking to some city fellow who would not appreciate a stranger's interest in his personal affairs. Sam had seen Tol get into some pretty tough spots. He was never sure that Tol ever realized that he was in a tough spot when he was in one; and Tol always got out of whatever tough spot he was in, and he never got out of it either by fighting or by shutting up. It was better than baseball, when Sam could maintain his detachment; when he couldn't, it was worse.

After the oysters, Tol would always have something or other he wanted to buy that he couldn't buy closer to home. And even if it wasn't but one thing, shopping for it would take exactly all the rest of the time they had.

*T*he time I am going to tell you about, Tol was looking for navy beans. He and Miss Minnie always grew a big garden and put up most of the stuff they needed, but something they never tried to grow was navy beans.

And so one of Tol's regular fall chores was to buy a two-bushel bag of them, which was usually enough to see them through the winter—some to keep and some to give away, according to the first rule of the Proudfoot household.

This year, Tol had found no navy beans in Port William and none in Hargrave. And so he made them the business of his and Sam's annual cattle-selling trip to Louisville. Sam followed him through the Haymarket, a couple of steps behind, picking his teeth, watching Tol with the patient interest with which a man already satisfied awaits further satisfaction.

Navy beans were scarce in Louisville, too, it turned out, for Tol visited all the likely places he knew without luck, and then they worked their way out into strange territory.

They finally went into a store that was not the sort of feed-and-seed establishment usually patronized by farmers, but a grocery store obviously set up to cater to the city trade—and, by the look of it, prosperous. There was a long wall of shelves full of canned goods, and a long counter in front of that, and in front of that a long row of wire baskets of fresh produce: potatoes, turnips, parsnips, eggs, cabbages, apples, and pears. In the back there were three fellows in suits—drummers, Sam thought—standing by a big iron stove, for it was cold that day. And behind the counter, talking to them, was a dapper fellow with a round face and round eyeglasses, his hair parted in the middle, garters on his sleeves, and a cigar in his mouth.

When Tol walked in with Sam behind him, the drummers and the clerk quit talking and looked. And they kept on looking. By that time, Sam said, Tol had been beyond the reach and influence of Miss Minnie long enough to look unusual. He looked as tall and wide as the door. He wore a sheepskin coat, unbuttoned, that flared out at the back and sides, giving the impression of great forward momentum. Half his shirttail was out. The bill of his next-best winter cap hovered between his right eye and his right ear. His britches legs were stuffed into the top of a pair of gum boots plastered with manure. He had bought a big sack of hard candy as a gift for Miss Minnie, and the twisted neck of the sack now stuck out as though he carried a setting goose in his pocket.

The three drummers and the proprietor looked at Tol. They watched him come back through the store, and then the drummers looked at each other and grinned. The proprietor watched Tol until he stopped and faced him across the counter.

"What can I do for you, Otis?" the proprietor asked. He never cracked a smile, but he gave the drummers just the slightest little wink, and the drummers chuckled.

None of them saw the look that crossed Tol's face, drawing one eye just a fraction of an inch narrower than the other, and if they had seen it they probably wouldn't have known what to make of it. But Sam, who was hanging back near the door, did see it, and did know what to make of it, and he made himself comfortable against the doorjamb and folded his arms.

Tol's eyes were set under bristly brows, and were much wrinkled at the corners. Mostly there was great candor in them; you could look through them right into his mind. But sometimes you could not see into his mind. At such times, thinking was going on in there that Tol didn't want anybody to find out about. When Tol thought, Sam Hanks said, he looked like he wasn't thinking at all; he looked like he was listening to a low rumble in his guts. And that was the way he looked for maybe about three seconds after the proprietor called him "Otis." And then, as if suddenly remembering where he was, he looked back at the proprietor.

"Two bushel of navy beans, if you got 'em, please, sir," said Ptolemy Proudfoot. If they had known their man, the proprietor and the drummers might have heard a very precise comment in the way Tol said "sir," but they missed that, too.

"I don't customarily sell them by the bushel, Timothy," the proprietor said, "but I believe I can let you have them."

"I'd be mightily obliged," said Tol.

The proprietor walked to a door in the back and called, "A bag of navy beans for Mr. Wheatly here."

Every time he called Tol by a new name, he glanced at the drummers, who seemed to be appreciating his wit a great deal, for they were grinning and nudging each other and whispering. And Sam appreciated it, too, in his way, for he knew as they did not that they were watching a contest.

A colored fellow came through the door in the back with the bag of beans on a hand truck and stood the bag up beside Tol.

The proprietor beat a little drumbeat on the edge of the counter with his hands. "Will that be all for you today, Mr. Bulltrack?"

"Well, I believe so," Tol said. "How much, if you please, sir?"

The proprietor told him, and Tol began grabbling in his pocket. He helped his suspenders with one hand and grabbled with the other, and finally drew out clenched in his fist an assortment of wadded bills, some coins, half a cut plug, a pocketknife, and the last three inches of a pencil. He made order of all this on one large stretched-out palm, and laid the price of the beans a bill or a coin at a time on the counter in front of the pro- prietor, the exact amount. And then he poked around in his hand and came up with a quarter.

He smiled over at the proprietor. "Ever see one of them disappear? I can make that disappear."

"Why, you're a magician, too, are you, Mr. Briarly?" the proprietor said, winking at the drummers. "Let me see."

Tol made a violent jerk with his right hand that

sent the coin bouncing to the floor between two baskets of produce. He got down, grunting, onto his hands and knees and laboriously retrieved it. The drummers were laughing out loud now, and the proprietor's face had begun to wear the smile of the successful host.

"He'd done lost me," Sam said. "Looked like he was *trying* to make a fool of himself. I thought, 'Now what?' "

"Well, you made it disappear, all right," the proprietor said.

"Wait a minute," Tol said, coming up with the quarter. "Watch it this time."

He made the same jerk, and sent the quarter spinning under the stove, and crawled after it. The drummers were holding onto themselves.

"Well, that ain't all the tricks I can do," Tol said. "I'll bet you this quarter I can jump into that basket of eggs and not break a one."

"Well, Spud, old boy, I'll just bet you can't," said the proprietor. And then he caught that look in Tol's eye that Sam had been watching all along, and his own eyes got wide. "Wup," he said.

He was too late. His lips had just shut on that little "wup" when Tol leapt into the air as light as a fox and came down with both feet in the basket of eggs. There was a loud crunch that totaled up the breaking of many small shells, and a viscous puddle began to spread slowly around the basket.

Tol's light leap and heavy descent were funny, Sam told me, but nobody laughed.

"Didn't you laugh?" I asked him.

"Hell, naw!" he said. "I was trying to act like I was there by myself. It was as quiet as a church with nobody in it. It was as quiet as a graveyard at midnight."

Tol stood in the basket of broken eggs with what Sam described as "a sweet, innocent smile," holding his quarter out to the proprietor. "Well, you got me. Dogged if you ain't a hard man to get ahead of."

The proprietor stood looking at Tol's quarter with his mouth open. "And then," Sam told me, "I swan if that fellow didn't reach out, still not quite able to get his mouth to shut, and take that quarter and put it in his pocket."

Tol stepped out of the basket, shouldered his sack of beans, and walked to the door, which Sam was holding open.

I heard Sam Hanks tell the story in town one July afternoon, and the next time I stopped by to see Miss Minnie, it occurred to me to ask her if she had ever heard it.

She had, of course. And she told it much as Sam had told it, but a good deal shorter. She was sitting in her rocker in the kitchen of the little house where she and Tol had passed the time their lives had been joined together. Now, their lives put asunder, Miss Minnie told the story with the mixture of approval and amusement with which she usually remembered Tol. When she finished the telling, she laughed. And then she sat in silence, reflecting, I knew, on the opposing claims of charity and justice in the story, and on the conflict of extravagance and gentleness in Tol's character. The late sun threw a patch of warm light on the wall behind her. The clock ticked.

"Mr. Proudfoot was that way," she said, and smiled. "But he was half sorry just as soon as he did it."

4 Nearly to the Fair

(1932)

In the neighborhood of Cotman Ridge and Goforth, and even as far away as Port William, Ptolemy Proudfoot had earned a small fame as a horseman. He never had need on his ninety-eight acres for more than three horses at once, and had rarely owned a brood mare; still, it was understood around and about that Tol was a good judge of horses and that he "had a way" with them. He was a good hand to break a colt, and he had been known to take an older horse that was spoiled or mean and settle him down to a life of useful citizenship. People knew that in his dealings with horses Tol could accomplish pretty much what he wanted or needed to, and without so much as raising his voice. "He was half horse himself," Sam Hanks liked to say.

He always kept as a work team a well-matched pair, usually of geldings, grays if he could find them. And he kept a somewhat lighter third horse that he drove to his buggy, and used with his team on the cutting harrow or breaking plow. The buggy horse, like the workhorses, would be a good one, and when Tol and Miss Minnie set out for town or for church, they traveled in some style. They looked, perhaps, as any moderately prosperous farm couple of that time and place would have looked, except for one thing. Tol, who was large in all dimensions, weighed in the neighborhood of three hundred pounds and Miss Minnie never more than about ninety, and so, when they traveled together in the buggy, the buggy leaned to Tol's side and Miss Minnie, as a consequence, always sat very close to Tol. Fortunately, Miss Minnie felt romantic about Tol—he was her bulwark, she said; it was not merely gravity that drew her to his side. But perhaps it was not ordinary in their time and place for a couple on the far side of middle age to sit as closely together as Tol and Miss Minnie did.

On his part, Tol's affection for Miss Minnie was always somewhat breathlessly mingled with awe. Miss Minnie had been a schoolteacher, and Tol looked up to her for her book learning and her correct grammar. For him, a certain romance adhered to their marriage because of his conviction that she was above him, that she deserved not only all he could do for her, but more.

And that, probably, is why he bought the little Model A coupe in 1929, just before the Depression. Tol, I think, would have been satisfied to stick to his horse and buggy for the rest of his days. Traveling in cooperation with a good horse interested him more than any other form of travel could have done. When they drove together he was in the habit of saying to Miss Minnie from time to time, gesturing toward Ike or Fiddler or Redbird or Sunfish or Hickory, "He's a good one, ain't he?" or "Stepping out now, ain't he?"—just as he liked often to say to her, when they had been away and had come back into sight of their neat gingerbreaded house and its outbuildings that stood just where the Cotman Ridge road dropped down toward Goforth in the valley, "Now I wonder who lives in *that* pretty place."

But Tol was no stranger to the fact that automobiles had come to be the thing. It got so that almost every time they went onto the road they met one—if it was good weather, that is, and the road was passable for automobiles. When they went down to Goforth to church, there several automobiles would be, not lined up at the hitch rail, but scattered hither and yon, not needing to be tied to anything when you were not using them. Even old Uncle Arn Ekrum had bought one; when it threatened to rust, he had covered it with a coat of whitewash so that now it looked like a ghost. And it came to Tol that Miss Minnie, abreast of things as he knew her to be, undoubtedly longed secretly in her heart to ride in an automobile of their own.

Tol could not bear the thought that Miss Minnie might long secretly in her heart for anything that he could provide. And so the next time they went to Hargrave—a trip they didn't make but two or three times

63

a year—Tol, speaking of a "surprise" he said he had for her, and revealing his own excitement by a smile that made his face shine like a ripe tomato, drove her to the place where a man sold automobiles and, stopping in front of a glossy Model A coupe, merely held out his hand, palm open, like Columbus presenting the New World to the Queen of Spain. And Miss Minnie—who despite Tol's suspicions had never dreamed of owning an automobile, who in fact loved Tol's way with a horse and loved to sit beside him while he drove, and who, now that she was suddenly face-to-face with a car of their own, thought it the homeliest black bug of a thing she had ever seen—assuming that it was something that Tol had longed for secretly in his heart, said, "Why, Mr. Proudfoot, it is perfectly beautiful!"

*T*he next day the salesman delivered the car and taught Tol how to drive it: how to start it by twisting its crank, how to guide it by twisting its steering wheel, how to make it go forward and backward. Tol did not know what to expect it to do next. But he got good enough finally to drive it three times slowly around the front pasture and then out the gate and down the road to Goforth, and then back up the hill and into the yard again, with the salesman beside him, smiling and saying, "You're getting the hang of it, sir. Just go easy."

And so Tol and Miss Minnie went easy into the

modern world, never really getting the hang of it. She
sat close to him in the Model A as she had in the buggy,
because of the same conditions of gravity and attraction.
And in the automobile, as in the buggy when the horse
trotted, she always held her hat on with one hand, even
when the windows were shut. All the neighbors, except
when they had to meet him in the road, enjoyed watching
the way Tol drove, as later they would enjoy remembering
it. When Tol traveled by horse and buggy, his horse
stayed in the road more or less on his own, leaving Tol
free to look around. Though the Model A required much
more supervision than a horse, Tol still spent a good deal
of time looking around. It would have seemed to him a
discourtesy to travel through the country without looking
at it. His course therefore involved a series of strayings
to one side or another, alternating with sudden corrections. The corrections were usually inspired by the warn-
ings of Miss Minnie, who always spoke in the nick of
time (who, on those journeys, *lived* in the nick of time),
and who nevertheless retained to the end of her days an
almost devout admiration of Tol's ability to run an
automobile.

Because they never entirely trusted their new machine, which Tol always referred to as "the Trick," and
because they had an almost superstitious fear of getting
it wet or muddy, they kept their horse and buggy for
use in emergencies and when the weather was bad and
when Tol needed to go somewhere by himself, for he

would not go anywhere in the Trick without Miss Minnie. And so the Model A stood in the wagon shed as innocent of rain or mud as a pet canary, and gleaming as on the day it was new, for Miss Minnie went over the outside of it almost every day with her dust mop.

Having an automobile might have caused them to think many thoughts that they had never thought before, but in fact it only caused one such thought. For the most part, they continued in their familiar, modest, frugal ways. They went to Port William to shop and visit a while on Saturday afternoon. They went down to Goforth to church on Sunday. They went to a neighbor's sometimes and sat till bedtime, or some of the neighbors would come to sit with them. And pretty often they would have company and Miss Minnie would load the table with one of her bountiful meals, and these were Tol's favorite occasions, for he loved food and talk and laughter. In the fall Tol would go to Hargrave to market his tobacco crop. He would go to the stockyards at Louisville in June to sell his lambs, and again in October or November to sell his steers. Occasionally Miss Minnie and the other women of the Missionary Society would hold a bake sale. But mostly she and Tol stayed home and stayed busy in the leisurely way of people who know exactly what they have to do and how to do it and have got used to doing it, and who don't have to do too much.

The one thought that the automobile caused them to think was the thought of the State Fair, which took place in Louisville at the end of every summer. They had heard of the Fair, and they had dreamed of it. They had heard of the perfect ears of corn laid side by side in rows, and of the perfect garden vegetables, the fruits and the canned goods, the needlework, the flowers; of the cages of beautiful chickens and ducks and geese, of guinea fowl and pigeons, of turkeys bronze and white; of ranks of fine cattle, and pens of excellent sheep and hogs; of the mule show and the horse show. Tol and Miss Minnie knew what good things were, and they had but to close their eyes to see them at the Fair as they must have been: all the produce of the cultivated earth, perfect in all its shapes and colors, cherished and gleaming. But they had never seen it with their own eyes. They had never gone.

But now that they possessed an automobile, they could think of going, for the world had changed. Now they could think of going fifty miles to the Fair and fifty miles home again on the same day, and only because they *wanted* to. It fairly took their breath. They talked about it for three years.

"If we wanted to go," Tol said prophetically to Miss Minnie, "the Trick could take us there."

"Yes, it's the modern world now," Miss Minnie replied. "People do such things."

But the truth was that in his heart Tol knew he belonged to an older world, and he was afraid. For him, to walk the aisles of the great exhibit halls among fruits and vegetables grown splendidly ripe, and to see the good animals fed and groomed to a royal excellence, would have been to set foot in Eden itself. But now, as never before, the thought of these things set off a tremor of anxiety in his mind. Getting there would be the problem.

And then one day something happened that enabled Tol Proudfoot to think of getting there. It was the middle of the summer, and Tol had walked through the field to Corbin Crane's to see if he could borrow back the corn planter that Corbin had borrowed from him in the spring. He thought that if he came walking, Corbin might offer to bring the planter home with his own team rather than wait, as he usually did, for Tol to come with his team to get it. Tol had thought it best to ask for the return of the planter several months ahead of time because if he knew Corbin, the planter would need fixing before it could be used. Corbin was hard on tools, as he was on everything else, which was perhaps why he saw fit to get along without any of his own.

He did, however, own a car. And when Tol came over the ridge, he saw the car running at what appeared to be terrific speed around the corner of the barn. It made a big loop in the pasture, disappeared again around the same corner of the barn, and reappeared in the lane, heading out toward the road gate. It disappeared again, and then in a few minutes it came back into sight, going backward nearly as fast as it had gone forward.

Tol, who had continued walking, stopped then and stood by the lane where it came up between the house and the barn. When the car flew backward past him, he hollered, "Whoa!" and the car stopped. Behind the wheel Tol saw his friend Elton Penn, Corbin Crane's stepson. Elton was twelve years old that summer, fairly big for his age, and as he raised his hand in greeting to Tol he had a grin on his face that Tol said could have been distributed among three or four boys and still showed them all to be in a good humor.

"Want a ride?" Elton said.

"Thanks. Not today," Tol said. "Where's Corbin?"

"Over to Braymer Hardy's, putting up hay," Elton said.

"Your mammy, too?"

Elton nodded.

"I thought so."

"They sent me home to milk."

"Well, why ain't you milking?"

Tol knew what Elton was doing. He was not just enjoying himself; he was taking revenge on Corbin Crane, who did not like him and was mean to him. It was because of Corbin's meanness to Elton that Tol and Elton had got to be friends.

One day Tol had stopped to talk to Corbin when Corbin and Elton were hoeing tobacco. While the two men talked, Elton, who was only about nine at the time, got to fiddling with the water jug, and he dropped it.

It didn't break, but some water spilled, and Corbin turned around and cracked Elton across the wrist with his hoe handle. It was a hard reckless lick, and Elton started to cry.

Tol heard no more of what Corbin was telling him. He reached down with his big old hand and picked up Elton's hand and led him away.

"If you don't mind," he said, not looking back at Corbin Crane, "I'm going to borrow this boy for a while."

They walked along together, Tol not saying anything, and Elton blubbering and sniffling. After a while Elton said, "Someday I'm going to kill that son of a bitch."

"Aw, son," Tol said, "you don't want to do that."

"I taken a shine to the boy," Tol told Miss Minnie later that day, meaning that from then on he was going to be Elton's friend.

And they were friends from then on. Tol would pay Elton a dime or a quarter to help him out with some little job. Or Miss Minnie would make cookies and lemonade, and they would call Elton on the party line to come over and play croquet. And often at night Tol would call Elton up and play Miss Minnie's Victrola for him over the telephone. A many a night Elton stood by the wall with the receiver to his ear, listening to "Mother Machree" or "There's a Cradle in Carolina" or, his and Tol's favorite, a song called "Nothing But Something Cool."

Once Tol offered Elton a dime to split a pile of stove wood. The wood split hard and the job took Elton a long time. Tol paid him his dime, and then showed him how to play the game of heads-or-tails.

"Now," Tol said, "look. If we bet a dime and you win, you'll have two dimes instead of one."

"All right," Elton said.

So they flipped.

"Call it," Tol Proudfoot said.

"Tails—wup—I mean heads!" Elton said.

And Tol showed his coin and took Elton's dime. Elton sat down on the pile of split wood and was not able to say anything, and Tol stood and looked down at him. After the suffering had gone on as long as Tol could stand it, he handed Elton back his dime.

"Son," he said, "don't never gamble."

And sometimes they just sat together while Tol told things.

One night, Tol said, when there was a full moon, he woke up, it must have been about three o'clock, and he could see Miss Minnie lying beside him on her back with her mouth open. Tol took the end of his forefinger and dabbled it into Miss Minnie's mouth and wiggled it around. And then he composed himself and breathed deeply. He heard Miss Minnie smacking her mouth. And then she sat straight up in bed.

"Mr. Proudfoot! Mr. Proudfoot, wake up! I have swallowed a mouse!"

"Miss Minnie," said Tol, his laughter shaking the bed so that, of course, she caught him, "there ain't much I know of to do for somebody that's swallowed a mouse."

Elton was a fine addition to Tol's and Miss Minnie's life. He liked them, they made him welcome, and it got so he would be over at their place whenever he could escape from home. He was a help. He didn't mind work, and he was bright. He saw things. He was interested in things. It often turned out that something Tol or Miss Minnie needed to have done and did not much want to do was something Elton was glad to do. He not only wanted to earn one of Tol's dimes or quarters and eat quite a lot of Miss Minnie's good cooking—he wanted to do the work. He seemed a godsend to Tol and Miss Minnie, who had no child of their own. They loved every little opportunity to pay attention to him. When he ate with them, they stuffed him like a sausage. Miss Minnie served him biscuits two at a time; when he bit into the second one, she popped two more hot ones onto his plate; while he buttered them, Tol would refill his glass. Miss Minnie baked pies and cookies for him, and brought him little snacks where he was at work.

When Tol saw how apt Elton was at driving a car, all his worry about getting to the Fair melted right out of his mind and flowed away. He saw that Elton, being young himself, belonged to the young world of machines. Whereas an old poot like Tol could drive an automobile only fearfully, and certainly with no skill, this Elton was already master of it, even at so young an age, and had no fear.

"Miss Minnie," Tol said, "the boy can drive. He can take us to the Fair."

And Miss Minnie said, "Oh, why didn't we think of that before?"

She thought and then added, "But, Mr. Proudfoot, won't it be too expensive?" They were then in the very pit of the Depression and, though she and Tol owed nothing and had savings, she felt it was appropriate to worry.

"Well," Tol said, "we ain't going probably but this once. If we figure in all the times we haven't gone and all the times we ain't going to go, it'll come out pretty cheap."

"It *would* be nice to go once," she said.

"You ought to see him go," Tol said. "That boy's worth a share in the railroad."

They secured Elton's agreement, broaching the subject with some care lest, after all, he might not want to undertake so daunting a project.

"Why, sure!" Elton said, grinning on behalf of himself and several others. "I imagine I can drive her."

They set the date. They told Elton to get permission from his folks.

And Elton did. Understanding the situation a good deal better than they did, Elton got permission from his folks to help Tol clean a fencerow on that day, which, as it happened, was a Saturday. He said he was supposed to stay overnight and go to church with Tol and Miss Minnie the next day, so he would need to take his Sunday clothes.

As a last precaution, Miss Minnie got her nephew Sam Hanks, who drove a cattle truck, to draw her a map showing how to get to the Fair. Sam sat between Tol and Miss Minnie at the kitchen table.

"Now here's the stockyards, Tol. You know how to get there."

"Aw, I know how to get *there*, all right!" Tol said.

"Well, starting from there, here's what you do." And Sam drew the streets onto a paper, telling them the various buildings and other landmarks by which they would recognize the turns, and they watched and listened and nodded their heads. He folded the map when he had finished and handed it to Miss Minnie, who laid it by her place at the table so she would remember to put it in her purse.

Sam had his doubts about Tol's driving. If they had had a bigger automobile, he might have offered to drive them himself, but he didn't favor being squeezed into that little coupe with Tol and Miss Minnie, and so he let it slide, only hinting a little warning to Tol.

"You'll be all right, now, won't you, Tol?"

"Sure."

"You sure?"

"Sure I'm sure."

If he had known their driver was to be a twelve-year-old boy, he surely would have interfered, but they didn't tell him, because he didn't ask. As for them, they just took for granted that if Elton could drive in a pasture, he could drive anywhere—and as it turned out, they were right.

*E*lton had to raise his chin to see over the dashboard, but under his guidance the Trick, as Tol Proudfoot pointed out to Miss Minnie, performed like a circus horse. They pulled out onto the road just as the sun was coming up. For the first dozen miles or so, they were on roads that were dry enough, but were chug-holey and narrow, and they had to go slow and be careful. And then they got onto the blacktop and just went whirling along, going faster by a good deal than Tol and Miss Minnie had ever gone in their lives. Elton drove with a big grin on his face, concentrating on his work, and Tol and Miss Minnie watched the country fly past and commented on what they saw. And every so often Tol would point out to Miss Minnie how splendidly Elton was driving.

Tol was having a wonderful time. For there they went, speeding through the world in the early morning, the Trick running as dependably as a good horse, but much faster; Tol had left his cares behind. And even though she had been a schoolteacher and felt a certain obligation to remain serious in the presence of the young,

Miss Minnie, too, felt the intoxication of their speed and became merry and carefree.

"I just wish you would look at that young man how he can drive!" Tol said. "Why, he can handle this Trick like he's a piece of it."

"I'm just the nut on the steering wheel," Elton said.

And Miss Minnie said, "Well, Mr. Nut, drive right on!"

That was when the left hind tire went "pish-pish-pish-pish," and Elton had to pull off on the side of the road.

Tol, who could do anything that needed doing with a horse and any of the tools he had been raised with, was utterly perplexed when confronted with a flat tire. Largely because of his eager help, it took Elton the better part of forty-five minutes to get the car jacked up and the impaired wheel off and the spare on and the car jacked back down again.

"Well, I don't expect we'll have any more flat tires today, do you?" Tol said when they were going again.

"There is no way to know what to expect," Miss Minnie said pleasantly but with a noticeable diminution of merriment. "We had better have that one fixed."

And so at the next service station they came to, they turned in. Only one man was working there, and he was busy, and they had to wait. There was a car ahead of them, also with a flat tire, and cars kept coming to the gas pump. It was getting hot now, and Tol and Elton got out to watch the mechanic while he worked, and Miss Minnie sat in the trick with her white-gloved hands crossed on top of her purse in her lap, the picture of patience.

When the mechanic started work on their tire, which gave them license to draw closer, Tol started passing the time of day with the mechanic. Commercial transactions embarrassed Tol. When he had to receive payment from somebody, the feeling would always come over him that it was too much; when he had to give payment, the same feeling would suggest that it was too little. The passage of money seemed to him to discount all else that might pass between people. And so he always strove to see to it that when the money finally had to pass, it would pass as if in secret under cover of much sociable conversation. And besides, he was interested in people and curious about them.

He found out the man's name, which was Bob Shifter. He found out where he lived, and where he had lived before. He found out that Bob Shifter was no kin to old man Claude Shifter who used to live close to Ellville down by Hargrave, or if he was he didn't know it. He found out how long Bob Shifter had been married and how many children he had. He found out the mechanic's wife's maiden name and his mother's maiden name. He found out all that and a lot more, and he didn't have to ask more than three or four direct questions, for Bob Shifter was more than glad to tell the story of his life, and not in much of a hurry, once the talk started, to fix the tire.

*T*he day was no longer young by the time they paid Mr. Shifter and got a good drink out of their water jug and started on again. But soon they were coming into the outskirts of the city. Now Tol began to experience their adventure as a reality, for the outskirts stretched out a long way before the city itself began. They would go through some of the city before they got to the stockyards, and there was a vast amount of it beyond.

He cleared his throat and said, "When you get me beyond the stockyards, by thunder, you've lost me!"

Nobody said anything.

After a while, to make sure they understood exactly what his qualifications were, he said again, "When you get me past the stockyards, I don't know left from right, nor up from down. I don't for a fact."

But by then they were approaching the stockyards, and Miss Minnie was digging in her purse for Sam Hanks's map.

"Now!" she said, drawing it out and unfolding it.

And then it was her turn to be assaulted by the reality of that day, for the map, past the stockyards, which had been boldly labeled "STOCKYARDS," did not have a single name on it. Beyond the stockyards, where they now were, and going past in a hurry, the map was just a squiggle of straight lines and right-angle turns. And Miss Minnie understood, in a sort of lightning flash, the urban experience of her well-traveled nephew: when he drove his truck in the city, he went by landmarks, even such landmarks as he had recited while he drew his map, causing her and Tol to see visions of where they were going; past the stockyards, he didn't know the name of anything.

"Well, there's an example of misplaced faith," said Miss Minnie in a voice that was precise and restrained and yet carried unmistakably the tone of familial exasperation.

They stopped for a red light and then went on again.

"What's the matter?" Tol said. Miss Minnie had never taken that tone with him, but he knew how he would have felt if she ever had, and so he felt sorry for Sam Hanks when she took it with him.

"There are no street names," Miss Minnie said. "The map is perfectly useless."

"Aw, naw, now, it's not," Tol said.

"I fear it is," said Miss Minnie.

"Well, it shows you where to turn," Tol said, putting his big forefinger down onto the paper. "Here. Look a-here. Right here. Turn!" he said to Elton, pointing the way.

And Elton turned left out of the middle of the great street they were on into a smaller one.

"Listen to all the horns," Tol said.

"If we don't know the names of the streets," Miss Minnie said, "how can we know where to turn?"

"Well, we just turn where the line turns," said Tol. "Keep a watch out now. Sam told us what to look for. Maybe he said the names of the streets. Maybe we'll remember some of them. Look at the signs."

So they began watching for the street signs. Miss Minnie was wearing a black straw hat with a stiff brim. "She was turning her head this way and that, looking for signs," as Elton would tell it later, "and that hat like to sawed off Tol's left arm and my head."

"Now," Tol said, "didn't he say to turn past that big building yonder?"

"Yes, perhaps he did," Miss Minnie said.

Elton turned, and they went along another street, and before long they turned again. They went on that way for a considerable time. Finally they could no longer be sure which of the anonymous angles on their map they had come to.

"Well," Miss Minnie said, "we're lost."

"Well, we know something for sure, anyhow," Tol said, and Miss Minnie allowed him to laugh at that all by himself.

"Why don't we ask somebody?" Elton said. "Looks like some of these people ought to know." Elton had never ceased to grin. He was having a good time. As long as he was driving, he didn't much care whether they were lost or not.

Miss Minnie, too, had thought of asking somebody, but she had her pride. If there was anything worse than being a person who did not know where she was, it was *appearing* to be a person who did not know where she was. Perhaps she understood also that by giving Tol an opening for conversation with the public at large, they might delay their arrival at the Fair indefinitely. And now that her confidence had failed, she saw pretty clearly that they would have to ask not one but many people. She saw that the place was complicated beyond her imaginings or her ability to imagine. She saw that even if they had good directions, they would get them wrong. There was no telling the mistakes they would make.

"It would be reasonable," she said, having calmly resolved to think it through again, "since the Fair is so large an event, that there ought to be signs along the way, saying, 'To the Fair.' And so perhaps if we just look around a little we will see one of those signs."

Buoyed up by the cheerfulness of logical thought, Tol agreed.

"And it seems to me," she said, pointing with her gloved forefinger, "that a promising direction would be *that* way."

And so they wandered about for a while, looking for a sign, and found none.

"Well," Tol said finally, "why don't we just look for a big street where a lot of people are going in the same direction. They'll probably be going to the Fair, for there's a many of them that goes. And we can just follow along. Don't you see?"

But it had got to where thinking did not much help either their spirits or their condition. And though they came to some more big streets, it appeared that about the same numbers of people were going in both directions.

"We must go back to the stockyards and begin again," Miss Minnie said.

And that was the worst thought of all, for only then did they understand how lost they were. That they did not know where they were suddenly proved to them that they did not know where the stockyards were. They did not know where home was.

Failure and despair came upon them. They could no longer say that they were on their way to the Fair. They had come to a place of railroad spurs, tall chimneys, and low buildings—a sooty, ugly, purposeful place that sunlight did not improve. And all the time they were wandering around lost, wasting their precious day, the Fair was happening; it was fleeing as a bird to its mountain. Miss Minnie had a vision of the light fading from the polished skins of apples and pears and plums.

"Oh, goodness!" she said, and Elton thought she was going to cry, but she did not.

And then a sort of wonder happened. Until he was about forty-five—when it was revealed to him that if he was going to get up early he ought to go to bed early—Tol Proudfoot had been a coon hunter, and so he was accustomed to being lost and to finding himself again. Once he understood that Miss Minnie herself was hopelessly bewildered, and that all rational measures had failed, Tol's sense of direction began to operate. "Now, the stockyards," he said, "if that's where we want to go, is right over yonder." And he pointed the direction.

It was a direction diagonal to the streets, and so they had to go in a zigzag, tacking back and forth like a sailboat.

"Slant her over that way a little, son," Tol would say. And then, in a little while, "Now cut her back over this way."

And finally they were going pretty fast, amid much traffic, down the middle of a long, broad street, and they could see, far down at the end of it, the stockyards. Tol was waving his hand, signaling to Elton to go straight ahead.

"Oh, Mr. Proudfoot!" said Miss Minnie. "Where would we be without you?"

And then, over on the left-hand side of the street, Tol spied a man on tall stilts, carrying a sandwich board that said:

You'll find it, friend,
At the Outside Inn.

It was perhaps the chief spectacle of the day so far. For fear the others would not see it, Tol lunged in the direction of the sandwich man and extended his hand to indicate where to look.

"Look a-yonder!" he said.

He had stuck his hand right in front of Elton's face. His hand looked as big, Elton said, as a billboard. And when they had seen the sandwich man and exclaimed and Tol withdrew his hand, the world had changed. The car in front of them was stopping in a hurry for a red light. Elton clapped his foot onto the brake. And what happened after that happened faster than it can be explained.

When the man in front applied his brake, as Elton would tell it, "his ass-end as-cended." When Elton applied his brake, which he did a little too late, the Trick's front end de-scended. And as everything stopped and got level again, the back bumper of the car in front chomped down onto the front bumper of the Trick.

Elton and Tol got right out to see what the damage was.

"It's all right," Elton said. "It didn't make a scratch."

But Tol Proudfoot knew a calamity when he saw one. "Hung like two dogs!" he said. "By thunder, son, they're hung like two dogs!"

The car in front was far longer and far shinier than the Trick. And now its driver had got out and come back to see also. He had a white mustache and a red face and was wearing a suit and was in a hurry.

Elton was grinning as if he could not wait for the world to show forth more of its wonders.

"What do you propose to *do* about this, sir?" the man said, and then, seeing that he addressed a mere boy, turned to Tol Proudfoot and said, *"Sir,* what do you propose to *do* about this?"

At that point the light turned green, and the traffic began to pour along on both sides of them, and behind them horns began to blow.

It seemed to Tol that the world, or anyhow his part of it, had come to an end, for he could see no way out. If he had any conviction still in force, it was that when a calamity has happened to somebody, other people ought to come to a respectful and helpful stop. But there he and Elton and Miss Minnie were, trapped and defeated beyond the power of a man to conceive, and nothing stopped. The cars and trucks and streetcars and wagons sped past, horns blew, and people shouted. The high, hot sun glared down into the crevice of the street without the mercy of a single tree.

He lifted his voice across their conjoined vehicles to the man with the mustache. "Hung like two dogs!" He spoke as sympathetically as he was able at the required volume, as if hoping to ease their predicament by so apt a description of it. He was sweating with heat and with panic. Behind him, in the trick, Miss Minnie's eyes were round and watery with unfallen tears, and her lips were shut tight together; her hands in their white gloves lay crossed over her purse in her lap and did not move.

"You must do something about this," the man shouted to Tol. "I don't have all day for this. I'm in a hurry!"

Tol then saw it through, as far at least as indignation. "Drive on!" he shouted back. "I reckon we can drag as fast as you can haul!"

That seemed to quiet the man, who obviously did not want to be accompanied anywhere by *them*.

Elton, who had been waving his hand for attention for some time, then said, "Mr. Tol, stand right here," and he pointed to the two stout brackets to which the Trick's bumper was attached.

"What?" Tol said.

"Stand on these!"

Elton showed him again. Propping himself on the back end of the other car, Tol clambered up onto the brackets, and the trick bowed down under his weight.

"Now take hold of that other bumper and lift up,"
Elton said.

When Tol lifted—which he did, Miss Minnie said,
"as with the strength of ten"—Elton applied himself with
all his strength to the left front fender of the trick, which
rolled back and came free. The man in a hurry, without
looking again at them, stepped back into his machine
and slammed the door.

Elton got back in behind the steering wheel. Tol,
whose conviction held further that all calamities should
be followed by conversation, stood in disappointment,
watching the other car drive away. And then he got in,
too.

"Well," Elton said, still grinning, "where does that
map say to go now?"

"Home, son." Tol Proudfoot laughed a little, as if
to himself, and patted Miss Minnie's crossed hands. "By
thunder, it says to go home."

"Yes," Miss Minnie said, "let us go home."

*T*hat is the story as I heard it many times from
Elton Penn—and from Sam Hanks, too, of course, for
he had his version of it, though Elton was its principal
eyewitness.

One day, when I happened by to see Miss Minnie,
it occurred to me to ask her about that famous trip. She
had been long a widow by then, and we neighbors often

made a point of happening by. We needed to know that she was all right, but also it was good for us to see her and to have her pleasant greeting.

"Oh, yes!" she said, when I brought the subject up. "We weren't able to get all the way to the Fair. We got *nearly* all the way. I'm sure it was wonderful. But we did succeed in getting all the way home. And wasn't Mr. Proudfoot happy to be here!"

5 *The Solemn Boy*

(1934)

*P*tolemy Proudfoot's ninety-eight-acre farm lay along the Goforth Hill road between the Cotman Ridge road and Katy's Branch. It included some very good ridgeland, some wooded hillside above the creek, and down beside the creek, on the other side of the Katy's Branch road, an acre or so of bottomland. This creek-bottom field, small and narrow and awkwardly placed, seemed hardly to belong to the farm at all, and yet it was the one piece of truly excellent land that Tol owned. He called it the Watch Fob. He kept it sowed in red clover and timothy or lespedeza and timothy, and every three or four years he would break it and plant it in corn.

Since the Watch Fob was so out of the way, whatever work Tol had to do there tended to be put off until last. And yet, such was the quality of the crops that came from that land, and such the pleasantness of the place, down among the trees beside the creek, that Tol always looked forward to working there. The little field was quiet and solitary. No house or other building was visible from it, and the road was not much traveled. When Tol worked there, he felt off to himself and satisfied. There were some fine big sycamores along the creek, and while Tol worked, he would now and then hear the cry of a shikepoke or a kingfisher. Life there was different from life up on the ridge.

Nineteen thirty-four was one of the years when Tol planted the Watch Fob in corn. And that was fortunate, for it was a dry year; the ridge fields produced less than usual, and the Watch Fob made up a good part of the difference. Tol cut and shocked that field last, and then he shucked and cribbed the upland corn before he went back again to the creek bottom.

Perhaps Tol agreed with the sage of Proverbs who held that "he that hasteth with his feet sinneth"—I don't know. It is a fact, anyhow, that Tol never hurried. He was not by nature an anxious or a fearful man. But I suspect that he was unhurried also by principle. Tol loved his little farm, and he loved farming. It would have seemed to him a kind of sacrilege to rush through his work without getting the good of it. He never went to the field without the company of a hound or two. At the time I am telling about, he had a large black-and-tan mostly hound named Pokerface. And when Tol went to work, he would often carry his rifle. If, while he was working, Pokerface treed a squirrel or a young ground-hog, then the workday would be interrupted by a little hunting, and Miss Minnie would have wild meat on the table the next day. When Tol went down to the Watch Fob to cultivate his corn, he always took his fishing pole. While he worked with plow or hoe, he would have a baited hook in the water. And from time to time he would take a rest, sitting with his back against a tree in the deep shade, watching his cork. In this leisurely way, he did good work, and his work was timely. His crops were clean. His pastures were well grassed and were faithfully clipped every year. His lambs and his steers almost always topped the market. His harvested corn gleamed in the crib, as clean of shuck and silk as if Tol had prepared it for a crowd of knowledgeable spectators, though as like as not he would be the only one who ever saw it.

By the time Tol got around to shucking the corn down on the Watch Fob that fall, it was past Thanksgiving. People had begun to think of Christmas. Tol had put off the job for two or three days, saying to himself, "I'll go tomorrow." But when he woke up on the morning he had resolved to go, he wished that he never had planted the Watch Fob in corn in the first place. Tol was sixty-two years old in 1934. He had not been young for several years, as he liked to say. And that morning when he woke, he could hear the wind ripping past the eaves and corners of the little farmstead, and rattling the bare branches of the trees.

"I'm getting old," he thought as he heaved his big

self off the mattress and felt beneath the bedrail for his socks.

"I'm getting old"—he had said that a number of times in the last few years, each time with surprise and with sudden sympathy for his forebears who had got old before him.

But he got up and dressed in the dark, leaving Miss Minnie to lie abed until he built up the fires. Tol was a big man. Clothing him, as Miss Minnie's nephew Sam Hanks said, was like upholstering a sofa. In sixty-two years Tol had never become good at it. In fact, putting on his clothes was an affair not in the direct line of his interests, and he did not pay it much attention. Later, while he sat with his coffee after breakfast and was thus within her reach, Miss Minnie would see that his shirt collar was turned down and that all his buttons had engaged the appropriate buttonholes.

Tol, anyhow, approximately dressed himself, went down the stairs, built up the fire in the living room, and lit a fire in the cooking range in the kitchen. He sat by the crackling firebox of the range, wearing his cap and coat now, and put on his shoes. And then he sat and thought a little while. Tol had always been a man who could sit and think if he had to. But until lately he had not usually done so the first thing in the morning. Now it seemed that his sixty-two years had brought him to a new place, in which some days it was easier to imagine staying in by the fire than going out to work. He had an ache or two and a twinge or two, and he knew without imagining that the wind was from the north and he knew how cold it was. Tol thought on these things for some time there by the warming stove, and he thought that of all his troubles thinking about them was the worst. After a while he heard Miss Minnie's quick footsteps on the floor upstairs. He picked up the milk buckets then and went to the barn.

A little later, having eaten a good breakfast and hitched his team to the wagon, Tol experienced a transformation that he had experienced many times before. He passed through all his thoughts and dreads about the day, emerging at last into the day itself, and he liked it.

The wind was still whistling down from the north over the hard-frozen ground. But his horses looked wonderful, as horses tend to do on such a morning, with every hair standing on end and their necks arched, wanting to trot with the wagon's weight pressing onto their breechings as they went down the hill, and their breath coming in clouds that streamed away on the wind. Tol's fingers grew numb in his gloves with holding them back.

They quieted down presently, and he drove on to the Watch Fob, sticking first one hand and then the other into his armpits to warm his fingers. And then he untied the first shock, slipped his shucking peg onto his right hand, and began tossing the clean yellow ears into the wagon. It was not yet full daylight. He settled into the work, so that presently he paid less attention to it, and his hands went about their business almost on their own. He looked around, enjoying the look of the little field. Even on so gray a day it was pretty. After he had cut and shocked the corn, he had disked the ground and sowed it in wheat, and now the shocks stood in their straight rows on a sort of lawn that was green, even though it was frozen. And it was pleasant to see the humanly ordered small clearing among the trees. Nearby the creek flowed under thin ice and then broke into the open and into sound as it went over a ripple and back again under ice. But the best thing of all was the quiet. Though he could hear the wind clashing and rattling in the trees around the rim of the valley, there was hardly a breeze down there in the Watch Fob. Surrounded by the wind's commotion, the quietness of the little cornfield gave it a sort of intimacy and a sort of expectancy. As his work warmed him, he unbuttoned his jacket. A while later he took it off.

A little past the middle of the morning, snowflakes began to fall. It was nothing at all like a snowstorm, but just a few flakes drifting down. Up on the ridgetops, Tol knew, the wind would be carrying the flakes almost straight across. "Up there," he thought, "it ain't one of them snows that falls. It's one of them snows that just passes by." But down where he was, the flakes sifted lackadaisically out of the sky as if they had the day off and no place in particular to go, becoming visible as they came down past the treetops and then pretty much disappearing when they lit. It would take hours of such snowing to make even a skift of whiteness on the ground. Pokerface, who in dog years was older than Tol, nevertheless took shelter under the wagon.

"Well, if *you* ain't something!" Tol said to him. "Go tree a squirrel."

Pokerface had a good sense of humor, but he did not appreciate sarcasm. He acknowledged the justice of Tol's criticism by beating his tail two or three times on the ground, but he did not come out.

There had been a time when a Proudfoot almost never worked alone. The Proudfoots were a big family of big people whose farms were scattered about in the Katy's Branch valley and on Cotman Ridge. They liked to work together and to be together. Often, even when a Proudfoot was at work on a job he could not be helped with, another Proudfoot would be sitting nearby to watch and talk. The First World War killed some of them and scattered others. Since then, the old had died and the young had gone, until by now Tol was the only one left. Tol was the last of the Proudfoots, for he and Miss Minnie had no children. And now, though he swapped work with his neighbors when many hands were needed, he often worked alone, amused or saddened sometimes to remember various departed Proudfoots and the old stories, but at other times just present there in the place and the day and the work, more or less as his dog and his horses were. When he was remembering he would sometimes laugh or grunt or mutter over what he remembered, and then the old dog would look at him and the horses would tilt their ears back to ask what he meant. When he wasn't remembering, he talked to the horses and the dog.

"Me and you," he said to Pokerface, "we're a fine pair of half-wore-out old poots. What are we going to do when we get old?"

It amused him to see that Pokerface had no idea either.

*F*or a while after Tol started that morning's work, it seemed to him that he would never cover the bottom of the wagon. But after he quit paying so much attention he would be surprised, when he did look, at how the corn was accumulating. He laid the stalks down as he snapped off the ears, and then when he had finished all the stalks, he stood them back up in a shock and tied them. The shucked ears were piling up nearly to the top of the wagon box by the time Tol judged it was getting on toward eleven o'clock. By then his stomach had begun to form the conclusion that his throat had been cut, as Proudfoot stomachs had always tended to do at that time of day. And now he began to converse with himself about how long it would take to get back up the hill and water and feed his horses. He knew that Miss Minnie would begin to listen for him at about eleven-thirty, and he didn't want to get to the kitchen much later than that. He thought that he *could* go in with what corn he had, but then he thought he might shuck just a *little* more. He had conducted thousands of such conversations with himself, and he knew just how to do it. He urged himself on with one "little more" after another until he filled the wagon properly to the brim, and in plenty of time, too.

The day was still cold. As soon as he quit work, he had to put his jacket back on and button it up. The thought of reentering the wind made him hunch his shoulders and draw his neck down into his collar like a terrapin.

He climbed up onto the wagon seat and picked up the lines. "Come here, boys," he said to the team. And they turned and drew the creaking load out of the field.

If Tol had a favorite thing to do, it was driving a loaded wagon home from the field. As he drove out toward the road, he could not help glancing back at the wagon box brimming with corn. It was a kind of wonder to him now that he had handled every ear of the load. Behind him, the little field seemed to resume a deeper quietness as he was leaving it, the flakes of snow still drifting idly down upon it.

When they started up the hill the horses had to get tight in their collars. It was a long pull up to the first bend in the road. When they got there, Tol stopped on the outside of the bend and cramped the wheels to let the horses rest.

"Take a breath or two, boys," he said.

"Come on, old Poke," he said to the dog, who had fallen a little behind, and now came and sat down proprietarily beside the front wheel.

Where they were now they could feel the wind. The snowflakes flew by them purposefully, as if they knew of a better place farther on and had only a short time to get there.

Pretty soon the cold began to get inside Tol's clothes. He was ready to speak to the team again when he heard Pokerface growl. It was a quiet, confidential growl to notify Tol of the approach of something that Pokerface had not made up his mind about.

When Tol looked back the way Pokerface was looking, he saw a man and a small boy walking up the road. Tol saw immediately that he did not know them, and that they were poorly dressed for the weather. The man was wearing an old felt hat that left his ears in the cold and a thin, raggedy work jacket. The boy had on a big old blue toboggan that covered his ears and looked warm, but his coat was the kind that had once belonged to a suit, not much to it, the lapels pinned shut at the throat. The sleeves of the boy's coat and the legs of his pants were too short. The man walked behind the boy, perhaps to shelter him a little from the wind. They both had their hands in their pockets and their shoulders hunched up under their ears.

"Hush, Poker," Tol said.

When the man and boy came up beside the wagon, the boy did not look up. The man glanced quickly up at Tol and looked away.

"Well," Tol said cheerfully, for he was curious about those people and wanted to hear where they came from and where they were going. "Can I give you a lift the rest of the way up the hill?"

The man appeared inclined to go on past without looking at Tol again.

"Give the boy a little rest?" Tol said.

The man stopped and looked at the boy. Tol could tell that the man wanted to let the boy ride, but was afraid or embarrassed or proud, it was hard to tell which. Tol sat smiling down upon them, waiting.

"I reckon," the man said.

Tol put down his hand and gave the boy a lift up onto the load of corn. The man climbed up behind him.

"We hate to put the burden on your team," the man said.

Tol said, "Well, it's all right. All they been doing is putting in the time. Get up, boys."

"They're right good ones," the man said.

Tol knew the man said that to be polite, but it was a pleasing compliment anyhow, for the man spoke as if he knew horses. Tol said, "They do very well."

And then he said, "You all come far?" hoping the man would tell something about himself.

But the man didn't. He said, "Tolable."

Tol glanced back and saw that the man had positioned his son between his spread legs and had opened his own coat to shelter him within it. As soon as he had stopped walking, the boy had begun to shiver. And now Tol saw their shoes. The man had on a pair of street shoes with the heels almost worn off, the boy a pair of brogans, too big for him, that looked as stiff as iron.

"Poor," Tol thought. Such men were scattered around the country everywhere, he knew—drifting about, wearing their hand-me-downs or grab-me-ups, looking for a little work or a little something to eat. Even in so out-of-the-way a place as Cotman Ridge Tol and Miss Minnie had given a meal or a little work to two or three. But till now they had seen no boy. The boy, Tol thought, was a different matter altogether.

Tol wanted to ask more questions, but the man held himself and the boy apart.

"That wind's right brisk this morning, ain't it?" Tol said.

"Tolable so," the man said.

"I'm Tol Proudfoot," Tol said.

The man only nodded, as if the fact were obvious.

After that, Tol could think of nothing more to say. But now he had the boy on his mind. The boy couldn't have been more than nine or ten years old—just a little, skinny, peaked boy, who might not have had much breakfast, by the look of him. And who might, Tol thought, not have much to look forward to in the way of dinner or supper either.

"That's my place up ahead yonder," he said to the man. "I imagine Miss Minnie's got a biscuit or two in the oven. Won't you come in and eat a bite with us?"

"Thank you, but we'll be on our way," the man said.

Tol looked at the boy then; he couldn't help himself. "Be nice to get that boy up beside the stove where he can get warm," he said. "And a bean or two and a hot biscuit in his belly wouldn't hurt him either, I don't expect."

He saw the man swallow and look down at the boy. "We'd be mighty obliged," the man said.

So when they came to his driveway, Tol turned in, and when they came up beside the house he stopped.

"You'll find Miss Minnie in the kitchen," Tol said. "Just go around to the back porch and in that way. She'll be glad to see you. Get that boy up close to the stove, now. Get him warm."

The man and boy got down and started around the back of the house. Tol spoke to his team and drove on into the barn lot. He positioned the wagon in front of the corncrib, so he could scoop the load off after dinner, and then he unhitched the horses. He watered them, led them to their stalls, and fed them.

"Eat, boys, eat," he said.

And then he started to the house. As he walked along he opened his hand, and the old dog put his head under it.

The man and boy evidently had done as he had told them, for they were not in sight. Tol already knew how Miss Minnie would have greeted them.

"Well, come on in!" she would have said, opening the door and seeing the little boy. "Looks like we're having company for dinner! Come in here, honey, and get warm!"

He knew how the sight of that little shivering boy would have called the heart right out of her. Tol and Miss Minnie had married late, and time had gone by, and no child of their own had come. Now they were stricken in age, and it had long ceased to be with Miss Minnie after the manner of women.

He told the old dog to lie down on the porch, opened the kitchen door, and stepped inside. The room was warm, well lit from the two big windows in the opposite wall, and filled with the smells of things cooking. They had killed hogs only a week or so before, and the kitchen was full of the smell of frying sausage. Tol could hear it sizzling in the skillet. He stood just inside the door, unbuttoning his coat and looking around. The boy was sitting close to the stove, a little sleepy looking now in the warmth, some color coming into his face. The man was standing near the boy, looking out the window—feeling himself a stranger, poor fellow, and trying to pretend he was somewhere else.

Tol took off his outdoor clothes and hung them up. He nodded to Miss Minnie, who gave him a smile. She was rolling out the dough for an extra pan of biscuits. Aside from that, the preparations looked about as usual. Miss Minnie ordinarily cooked enough at dinner so that there would be leftovers to warm up or eat cold for supper. There would be plenty. The presence of the two strangers made Tol newly aware of the abundance, fragrance, and warmth of that kitchen.

"Cold out," Miss Minnie said. "This boy was nearly frozen."

Tol saw that she had had no luck either in learning who their guests were. "Yes," he said. "Pretty cold."

He turned to the little washstand beside the door, dipped water from the bucket into the wash pan, warmed it with water from the teakettle on the stove. He washed his hands, splashed his face, groped for the towel.

As soon as Tol quit looking at his guests, they began to look at him. Only now that they saw him standing up could they have seen how big he was. He was broad and wide and tall. All his movements had about them an air of casualness or indifference as if he were not conscious of his whole strength. He wore his clothes with the same carelessness, evidently not having thought of them since he put them on. And though the little boy had not smiled, at least not where Tol or Miss Minnie could see him, he must at least have wanted to smile at the way Tol's stiff gray hair stuck out hither and yon after Tol combed it, as indifferent to the comb as if the comb had been merely fingers or a stick of wood. But when Tol turned away from the washstand, the man looked back to the window and the boy looked down at his knee.

"It's ready," Miss Minnie said to Tol, as she took a pan of biscuits from the oven and slid another in.

Tol went to the chair at the end of the table farthest from the stove. He gestured to the two chairs on either side of the table. "Make yourself at home, now," he said to the man and the boy. "Sit down, sit down."

He sat down himself and the two guests sat down.

"We're mighty obliged," the man said.

"Don't wait on me," Miss Minnie said. "I'll be there in just a minute."

"My boy, reach for that sausage," Tol said. "Take two and pass 'em.

"Have biscuits," he said to the man. "Naw, that ain't enough. Take two or three. There's plenty of 'em."

There was plenty of everything: a platter of sausage, and more already in the skillet on the stove; biscuits brown and light, and more in the oven; a big bowl of navy beans, and more in the kettle on the stove, a big bowl of applesauce and one of mashed potatoes. There was a pitcher of milk and one of buttermilk.

Tol heaped his plate, and saw to it that his guests heaped theirs. "Eat till it's gone," he said, "and don't ask for nothing you don't see."

Miss Minnie sat down presently, and they all ate. Now and again Tol and Miss Minnie glanced at one another, each wanting to be sure the other saw how their guests applied themselves to the food. For the man and the boy ate hungrily without looking up, as though to avoid acknowledging that others saw how hungry they were. And Tol thought, "No breakfast." In his concern for the little boy, he forgot his curiosity about where the two had come from and where they were going.

Miss Minnie helped the boy to more sausage and more beans, and she buttered two more biscuits and put them on his plate. Tol saw how her hand hovered above the boy's shoulder, wanting to touch him. He was a nice-looking little boy, but he never smiled. Tol passed the boy the potatoes and refilled his glass with milk.

"Why, he eats so much it makes him poor to carry it," Tol said. "That boy can put it away!"

The boy looked up, but he did not smile or say anything. Neither Tol nor Miss Minnie had heard one peep out of him. Tol passed everything to the man, who helped himself and did not look up.

"We surely are obliged," he said.

Tol said, "Why, I wish you would look. Every time that boy's elbow bends, his mouth flies open."

But the boy did not smile. He was a solemn boy, far too solemn for his age.

"Well, we know somebody else whose mouth's connected to his elbow, don't we?" Miss Minnie said to the boy, who did not look up and did not smile. "Honey, don't you want another biscuit?"

The men appeared to be finishing up now. She rose and brought to the table a pitcher of sorghum molasses, and she brought the second pan of biscuits, hot from the oven.

The two men buttered biscuits, and then, when the butter had melted, laid them open on their plates and covered them with molasses. And Miss Minnie did the same for the boy. She longed to see him smile, and so did Tol.

"Now, Miss Minnie," Tol said, "that boy will want to go easy on them biscuits from here on, for we ain't got but three or four hundred of 'em left."

But the boy only ate his biscuits and molasses and did not look at anybody.

And now the meal was ending, and what were they going to do? Tol and Miss Minnie yearned toward that nice, skinny, peaked, really pretty little boy, and the old kitchen filled with their yearning, and maybe there was to be no answer. Maybe that man and this little boy would just get up in their silence and say, "Much obliged," and go away, and leave nothing of themselves at all.

"My boy," Tol said—he had his glass half-full of buttermilk in his hand, and was holding it up. "My boy, when you drink buttermilk, always remember to drink from the near side of the glass—like this." Tol tilted his glass and took a sip from the near side. "For drinking from the far side, as you'll find out, don't work anything like so well." And then—and perhaps to his own surprise—he applied the far side of the glass to his lips, turned it up, and poured the rest of the buttermilk right down the front of his shirt. And then he looked at Miss Minnie with an expression of absolute astonishment.

For several seconds nobody made a sound. They all were looking at Tol, and Tol, with his hair asserting itself in all directions and buttermilk on his chin and his shirt and alarm and wonder in his eyes, was looking at Miss Minnie.

And then Miss Minnie said quietly, "Mr. Proudfoot, you *are* the limit."

And then they heard the boy. At first it sounded like he had an obstruction in his throat that he worked at with a sort of strangling. And then he laughed.

He laughed with a free, strong laugh that seemed to open his throat as wide as a stovepipe. It was the laugh of a boy who was completely tickled. It transformed everything. Miss Minnie smiled. And then Tol laughed his big hollering laugh. And then Miss Minnie laughed.

And then the boy's father laughed. The man and the boy looked up, they all looked full into one another's eyes, and they laughed.

They laughed until Miss Minnie had to wipe her eyes with the hem of her apron.

"Lord," she said, getting up, "what's next?" She went to get Tol a clean shirt.

"Let's have some more biscuits," Tol said. And they all buttered more biscuits and passed the molasses again.

When Miss Minnie brought the clean shirt and handed it to him, Tol just held it in his hand, for he knew that if he stood up to change shirts the meal would end, and he was not ready for it to end yet. The new warmth and easiness of their laughter, the straight way they all had looked at one another, had made the table a lovely place to be. And he liked the boy even better than he had before.

Tol began to talk then. He talked about his place and when he had bought it. He told what kind of year it had been. He spoke of the Proudfoots and their various connections, and wondered if maybe his guests had heard of any of them.

No, the man said, he had never known a Proudfoot until that day. He went so far as to say he knew he had missed something.

Tol then told about marrying Miss Minnie, and said

that things had looked up around there on that happy
day, which caused Miss Minnie to blush. Miss Minnie
had come from a line of folks by the name of Quinch.
Had their guests, by any chance, ever run into any
Quinches?

But the man said no, there were no Quinches where
he came from.

Which brought Tol to the brink of asking the man
point-blank where he came from and where was he going.
But then the man retrieved his hat from under his chair,
and so put an end to all further questions forever, leaving
Tol and Miss Minnie to wonder for the rest of their lives.

The man stood up. "We better be on our way," he
said. "We're much obliged," he said to Tol. "It was
mighty fine," he said to Miss Minnie.

"But wait!" Miss Minnie said. Suddenly she was all
in a flutter. "Wait, wait!" she said. "Don't go until I
come back!"

She hurried away. All three of them stood now,
saying nothing, for a kind of embarrassment had come
over them. Now that the meal had ended, now that they
had eaten and talked and laughed together for a moment,
they saw how little there was that held them. They heard
Miss Minnie's footsteps hurry into the front of the house
and up the stairs. And then they heard only the wind
and the fire crackling quietly in the stove. And then they
heard her footsteps coming back.

When she came into the kitchen again, she was

carrying over her left arm an old work jacket of Tol's, and holding open with both hands a winter coat of her own that she had kept for second best. She put it on the boy, who obediently put his arms into the sleeves, as if used to doing as a woman told him.

But when she offered the work jacket to the man, he shook his head. The jacket was much patched, worn and washed until it was nearly white.

"It's old, but it's warm," Miss Minnie said.

"No, mam," the man said. For himself, he had reached some unshakable limit of taking. "I can't take the jacket, mam," he said. "But for the boy, I thank you."

He started toward the door then. Miss Minnie hurriedly buttoned the boy into the coat. Tol made as if to help her by prodding the coat here and there with his fingers feeling between the weather and the boy's skinny back and shoulders the reassuring intervention of so much cloth.

"It's not a fit exactly, but maybe it'll keep him warm," Miss Minnie said as if only to herself. The coat hung nearly to the top of the boy's shoes. "It's good and long," she said.

Her hands darted about nervously, turning the collar up, rolling up the sleeves so that they did not dangle and yet covered the boy's hands. She tucked the boy into the coat as if she were putting him to bed. She snatched a paper bag from a shelf, dumped the remaining biscuits into it out of the pan, and at the last moment, before letting the boy go, shoved the sack into the right-hand pocket of the coat. "There!" she said.

And then they lifted their hands and allowed the boy to go with his father out the door. They followed. They went with the man and boy around the back of the house to the driveway.

The man stopped and turned to them. He raised his hand. "We're mightily obliged," he said. He turned to Miss Minnie, "We're mightily obliged, mam."

"You might as well leave that boy with us," Tol said. He was joking, and yet he meant it with his whole heart. "We could use a boy like that."

The man smiled. "He's a good boy," he said. "I can't hardly get along without this boy."

The two of them turned then and walked away. They went out to the road, through the wind and the gray afternoon and the flying snow, and out of sight.

Tol and Miss Minnie watched them go, and then they went back into the house. Tol put on the clean shirt and his jacket and cap and gloves. Miss Minnie began to clear the table. For the rest of that day, they did not look at one another.

*T*ol lived nine more years after that, and Miss Minnie twenty more. She was my grandmother's friend, and one day Granddad left Granny and me at the Proudfoot house to visit while he went someplace else. The war was still going on, and Tol had not been dead a year. I sat and listened as the two women talked of the time and of other times. When they spoke of the depression, Miss Minnie was reminded of the story of the solemn boy, and she told it again, stopping with Tol's words, "We could use a boy like that."

And I remember how she sat, looking down at her apron and smoothing it with her hands. "Mr. Proudfoot always wished we'd had some children," she said. "He never said so, but I know he did."

6 *Turn Back the Bed*

(1941)

To some, it seemed that Ptolemy Proudfoot didn't *laugh* like a Christian. He laughed too loud and too long, and his merriment seemed just a little too self-sufficient—as if, had there been enough funny stories and enough breath to laugh at them with, he might not *need* to go to Heaven.

What tickled him as much as anything were his own stories about his grandfather, Mark Anthony Proudfoot, known as Ant'ny and later, of course, as Old Ant'ny. Old Ant'ny was, you might say, the Tol Proudfoot of his generation, with a few differences, the main one being that whereas Tol was childless, Old Ant'ny sired a nation of Proudfoots. Once his progeny had grown up and acquired in-laws and produced scions of their own, they seemed as numerous as the sand which is upon the sea shore.

The great events of Tol's boyhood were the family gatherings that took place three or four times a year at

113

Old Ant'ny's place above Goforth in the Katy's Branch valley. By that time Ant'ny was in his old age. He had always been a big man, and now, with less activity and no loss of appetite, he had grown immense. He sat at these meetings, as massive and permanent-seeming almost as the old log house itself, holding a cane in his hand, seldom stirring from the chair that one of his sons had constructed for him out of poplar two-by-fours. He sat erect and mostly in silence, looking straight ahead, his white beard reaching down to his fourth shirt button. Now and then he would say something in a rolling deep voice that whoever was in the room would stop and listen to. And now and then he would reach out with his cane and hook a passing grandson or great-grandson, whose name and the name of whose parents he would demand to know. But for the most part he sat in silence, shedding his patriarchal influence over a circumference of about six feet, while round him the fruit of his loins revolved, battering floor and walls, like a storm.

Old Ant'ny was a provider, and he did provide. He saw to it that twelve hogs were slaughtered for his own use every fall—and twenty-four hams and twenty-four shoulders and twenty-four middlings and twenty-four spareribs and twelve backbones and hard to say how many sacks of sausage were hung in his smokehouse. And his wife, Maw Proudfoot, kept a flock of turkeys and a flock of ducks and geese and a flock of guineas, and her henhouse was as populous as a county seat. And long after he was "too old to farm," Old Ant'ny grew a garden as big as some people's crop. He picked and dug and fetched, and Maw Proudfoot canned and preserved and pickled and salted as if they had an army to feed—which they more or less did, for there were not only the announced family gatherings but always somebody or some few happening by, and always somebody to give something to.

The Proudfoot family gatherings were famous. As feasts, as collections and concentrations of good things, they were unequaled. Especially in summer there was nothing like them, for then there would be old ham and fried chicken and gravy, and two or three kinds of fish, and hot biscuits and three kinds of cornbread, and potatoes and beans and roasting ears and carrots and beets and onions, and corn pudding and corn creamed and fried, and cabbage boiled and scalloped, and tomatoes stewed and sliced, and fresh cucumbers soaked in vinegar, and three or four kinds of pickles, and if it was late enough in the summer there would be watermelons and muskmelons, and there would be pies and cakes and cobblers and dumplings, and milk and coffee by the gallon. And there would be, too, half a dozen or so gallon or half-gallon stone jugs making their way from one adult male to another as surreptitious as moles. For in those days the Proudfoot homeplace, with its broad cornfields in the creek bottom, was famous also for the excellence of its whiskey.

So of course these affairs were numerously attended. When the word went out to family and in-laws it was bound to be overheard, and people came in whose veins Proudfoot blood ran extremely thin, if at all—and some came who were not even speakingly acquainted with so much as a Proudfoot in-law. And there would be babel and uproar all day, for every door stood open, and the old house was not ceiled; the upstairs floorboards were simply nailed to the naked joists, leaving cracks that you could not only hear through but in places see through. Whatever happened anywhere could be heard everywhere.

The storm of feet and voices would continue unabated from not long after sunup until after sundown when the voice of Old Ant'ny would rise abruptly over the babbling of the multitude: "Well, Maw, turn back the bed. These folks want to be gettin' on home." And then, as if at the bidding of some Heavenly sign, the family sorted itself into its branches. Children and shoes and hats were found, identified, and claimed; horses were hitched; and the tribes of the children of Old Ant'ny Proudfoot set out in their various directions in the twilight.

*I*n himself and in his life, Tol Proudfoot had come a considerable way from the frontier independence and uproariousness of Old Ant'ny's household. He was a gentler, a more modest, perhaps a smarter man than his grandfather. And he had submitted, at least somewhat, to the quieting and ordering influence of Miss Minnie. But there was something in Tol, in his spirit as well as in his memory, that hung back there in the time of those great family feasts, which had been a godsend to every boy, at least, who ever attended one.

By the time I came to know him, Tol was well along in years. He had become an elder of the community, and had recognized his memories, the good ones anyhow, as gifts, to himself and to the rest of us. His stories of Old Ant'ny and the high old family times were much in demand, not just because they were good to listen to in their own right, but because certain people enjoyed hearing—and watching—Tol laugh at them. Once he got tickled enough, you could never tell what would happen. He had broken the backs off half a dozen chairs, rearing back in them to laugh. Once, at an ice cream supper, he fell backward onto a table full of cakes.

My grandparents took me to a picnic one Sunday at the Goforth church where Tol and Miss Minnie went. After the morning service, the women spread the food out on tables under the big old oak trees in the church-yard, and then we gathered around and sang "Blessed Be the Tie that Binds," and the minister gave thanks for the food, and we ate together, some finding places at the tables, some sitting in the shade of the trees, holding their plates on their laps.

Afterward the men drew off to themselves, carrying

their chairs up to the edge of the graveyard. There was a good breeze there on the higher ground, and fine dark shade under the cedars. They took smokes and chews, and the talk started, first about crops and weather and then about other things. I don't remember exactly how, but a little merriment started. Then somebody said, "Tol, tell that un about Old Ant'ny and the chamber pot."

They were sitting more or less in a circle in the shade of two big cedars, and in the silences you could hear the breeze pulling through the branches. Tol was sitting with his back to the graveyard, his chair tilted back, the gravestones spread out behind him. He had outlived nearly everybody he would tell about, some of whom lay within the sound of his voice, and he was sitting not far from the spot where we would lay him to rest before two more years had passed.

Below us the women were sitting together near the tables, where they had finished straightening up. You could hear the sound of their voices but not what they said. I remember the colors of their dresses: white and pink and yellow, ginghams and flower prints; the widows all in black, the dresses of the older women reaching to their ankles. And I remember how perfect it all seemed, so still and comfortable. The Second World War had started in Europe, but in my memory it seems that none of us yet knew it.

Tol's pipe was lit, and he had picked up a dead

cedar branch to whittle. His knife was sharp, and the long, fine, fragrant shavings curled and fell backward over his wrists. He was smiling.

"Boys," he said, "I couldn't tell it all in a day."

He laughed a little and said no more. Nobody else said anything either. After a minute he began to tell the story. I wasn't anything but a boy then. I can't tell it the way he told it, but this is the way he put it in my mind:

It was a fine, bright Sunday in October, the year Tol was five years old. The Proudfoots had gathered at Old Ant'ny's. The family had drawn in its various branches, outposts, in-laws, and acquaintances, as well as the usual sampling of strangers. Old Ant'ny had turned out his own mules and horses to make stall room, and by midmorning the barn was full, and saddled horses and harnessed teams stood tied to fence posts.

All the wives had brought food and other necessaries to add to the bounty already laid in and prepared by Old Ant'ny and Maw Proudfoot, and the big kitchen and back porch were full of women and the older girls, setting out dishes and pitchers and glasses and bowls on tables spread with white cloths.

The Proudfoot men were gathered around the hearth in the living room, where Old Ant'ny sat and where in the early morning there had been a fire. Later, as their numbers grew and the day warmed, some of them sat along the edge of the front porch, and others squatted in the open doorway of the barn.

The girls who were too little to help played or visited quietly enough with each other. They were well acquainted, happy to be together again, and possessed of a certain civility and dignity. There was never much trouble from them.

The trouble came from the boys, or, more exactly, from the boys between the ages of about five and about eleven, who did not come with any plans or expectations, and who therefore took their entertainment as a matter of adventure, making do with whatever came to hand. There were, Tol said, "a dozen, maybe twenty" of them.

Before dinner they were kept fairly well under control. They were getting hungry, for one thing, and that held them close to the house. For another thing, the parents were more alert before dinner than they would be afterward. Afterward, they would be full and comfortable and a little sleepy, and most of the men would be a little sleepier and more comfortable than the women, for by then they would have tested some stealthily wandering jug of Old Ant'ny's whiskey.

That was the way it always worked. During the morning the boys were kept within eyesight of the grownups, and pretty well apart from each other. They fretted and jiggled and asked when dinner would be ready, and got corrected and fussed at and threatened. And then after dinner the range of grown-up eyesight shortened, and that was when the boys got together and began to run. This was their time of freedom, and to preserve it they ran. Whenever they were near the house, where they knew they might be seen and called down, they ran. They ran in a pack, the big ones in front, the little ones behind. Tol was the littlest one that year, and the farthest behind, but he kept the rest of them in sight. Most of them were Proudfoots, and they all looked more or less like Proudfoots. And as long as there were so many of them and they were all running, by the time one of them could be recognized and called to, they would be gone.

They ran up the hill behind the barn and over into a wooded draw where their band raveled out into a game of tag, and then a game of hide-and-go-seek—a great crashing and scuffling in the fallen dry leaves. The biggest boy that year was Tol's cousin Lester, whose hair, plastered down with water early that morning, now stuck up like the tail of a young rooster, and whose eyes were wide open in expectation.

Tag and hide-and-go-seek didn't last long. Lester kept changing the rules until nobody wanted to play. Then Old Ant'ny's hounds treed a groundhog in a little slippery elm, and Lester climbed up to shake him out. Lester took his jacket off so he could climb better. When he threw it down, the dogs, thinking it was the groundhog, piled on it and tore it up. While they were tearing up Lester's jacket, the groundhog jumped out of the tree and ran into a hole. The big boys found a couple of sticks and helped the dogs dig until they came to a rock ledge and had to give up.

All that took a while. They had been missed by then, and Aunt Belle was on the back porch, calling, "Oh, Lester!" So they answered and went back, running, allowing themselves to be seen and forgotten again, and ran on across the cornfield to the creek.

They played follow-the-leader, which lasted a long time, because Lester was the leader. They went along the rocks at the edge of the creek and then waded a riffle and came back across walking a fallen tree trunk. And then Lester said, "Follow my tracks," and started taking giant steps across a sand bar. It was a long straddle, and by the time Tol got there the tracks were a foot deep and full of water. He got stuck with his feet apart and fell over sideways.

"Come here, mud man," Lester said. "Come here, mud boy." And he soused Tol, clothes and all, down into the deep cold water and rinsed him off.

Tol started crying. He said a word he had learned from Uncle O.R. and threw a rock at Lester, and everybody laughed, and then Tol did.

Aunt Belle was on the front porch now, hollering again. She was a big woman with a strong voice. Lester answered and they all started running back toward the house, leaving Tol behind. He was getting tired, and so

he walked on to the house. When he got there the other
boys were gone again, out of sight. He went up on the
back porch, taking care to avoid notice, and found a plate
of biscuits under a cloth on the wash table and took two
and went on toward the front door. The women were in
the kitchen and in the parlor, talking. Old Ant'ny and
Uncle O.R. and Uncle George Washington and Uncle
Will and Uncle Fowler and some others were in the living
room. A brown and white jug, stoppered with a corncob,
was sitting by Uncle Fowler's chair like a contented cat.
They weren't going to pay any attention to Tol, and he
stepped inside the door to eat his biscuits. Uncle Fowler
leaned forward in his chair to spit in the fireplace and
fell headfirst into the ashes. Old Ant'ny never even
looked. The others may have looked or they may not.
They never said anything. But Uncle O.R. looked. He
was standing on the corner of the hearth, leaning one
shoulder against the mantel. He said, "Fowler, you're
putting a right smart effort into your spitting, seems
like."

Uncle Fowler got himself out of the ashes and into
his chair again. "Whoo, Lordy, Lordy!" he said, and
fanned himself with his hand, causing a few ashes to float
out of his mustache.

Tol crammed the whole second biscuit into his
mouth, and ran back through the house and out the back
door, blowing crumbs ahead of him as he ran.

Lester was up on the roof. He had climbed up on the cellar, and then onto the cellar house roof, and then onto the back porch roof, and then onto the roof of the ell that held the kitchen and dining room, and now he was walking up the slope of the roof over the living room and the bedroom above it toward the chimney. Maw Proudfoot's yellow tomcat was weaving in and out between Lester's feet, stroking himself on Lester's legs. The pack of boys had backed up as Lester climbed, keeping him in sight.

It was a big rock chimney built against the end of the house. Lester reached into it, and held up a black palm for the others to see. The yellow cat climbed up onto the chimney beside Lester. He walked back and forth along the copestones, rubbing himself against Lester's shoulder, his tail stuck straight up, with a little crook on the end of it like a walking cane.

It was past sundown now. The light was going out of the sky, and it was turning cool. Except for the pack of boys, everybody was in the house. Nobody had started home yet. They would get home in the dark and still have the milking to do; maybe the thought of that had quieted them. The old house hovered them now like a mother hen.

Lester backed away a step, and he and the yellow cat stood looking at each other, balanced across the foot or so of air that divided them. Some fascination grew

upon them. The boys watching down in the yard felt it.
And then Lester raised his hand and gave a little push.

When Lester pushed the cat, he said, "Wup!"

The cat disappeared, clean out of sight, as if the
sky had bitten it off. They heard a fit of scratching inside
the chimney, and then it ceased. Lester looked over into
the chimney mouth. And then he looked around and
down at his cousins. His eyes were as wide open as if he
had never batted one of them once in his life.

"He didn't go all the way down," Lester said. "He
ain't going to make it back up."

Lester looked down at his cousins, and they looked
up at him. Nobody moved or spoke. For maybe as long
as a minute, nobody had any idea what would happen
next. And then Lester's eye fell on Toby.

Several hounds were sitting alongside the pack of
boys, watching too, with the same balked expectancy,
and Toby was with them. Toby was Old Ant'ny's feist,
white with black ears and a black spot in front of his
tail. He was a nervous little dog who had courage instead
of brains. He would fight anything, would go unhesi-
tatingly into a hole after a varmint, or anywhere after a
cat.

"Send up old Tobe," Lester said.

One of the older boys put Toby in the crook of his
arm and carried him up onto the kitchen roof. Lester met

him and took the dog. He went back up to the chimney and held Toby so he could look in. He might have intended just to show Toby to the cat so as maybe to scare the cat into going on down. Tol didn't know. But whatever Lester intended to do turned out to be beside the point. When the cat saw Toby, he spit at him. They could hear it all the way down in the yard. Toby gave a little yelp, in horror of what he saw he was about to do, and jumped out of Lester's arms onto the lip of the chimney and down onto the cat.

The boys had already started running before Toby jumped. When they passed the chimney, they heard Toby and the cat inside, falling and fighting.

They went on around and through the front door and into the living room just in time to see the ashes in the fireplace rise up in a cloud. And then the cat, with Toby behind him, broke out and ran up Uncle Fowler's leg and up his belly and up over the top of his head and off the back of his chair and through the crowd of boys and out into the hall. Old Ant'ny never looked, never turned his head. He just sat there like some people's idea of God, as if having set this stir in motion, he would let it play itself out on its own, as if he despaired of any other way of stopping it. Uncle Fowler, who had been asleep, woke up, spitting ashes, just as Toby cleared the chair back.

"Pew!" Uncle Fowler said. He sighed and shut his eyes again in great weariness.

The only one with enough presence of mind to move at all was Uncle O.R., who started out, running after Toby, only to get tangled up in the crowd of boys standing in the door.

The cat treed under the chiffonier in the hall, but Toby brought him out of there, and by the time Uncle O.R. got free of the boys, the cat had run into the kitchen and down the middle of the table, with Toby still on his heels, and over Aunt Belle's shoulder and out the window. They left a black streak down the middle of the cloth.

Aunt Belle was on her feet now. "Who the *hell* let that cat in? And that *damn* dog? *Where* are you, Lester?"

Uncle O.R. ran on out through the kitchen. The pack of boys, who had been following Uncle O.R., got to the dining room door just in time to run smack into Aunt Belle who was coming out. She was red in the face and already puffing; she just bounced them all out of the way and ran on up the hall toward the front door. They fell in behind her, running as dutifully as if they were all still playing follow-the-leader.

Aunt Belle ran out the front door and across the porch and down the porch steps and out in the yard just as Lester came around the corner of the house with Uncle O.R. gaining on him. Lester's eyes were wider open than ever, his hair was sticking up stiff and straight.

Aunt Belle was still running, too. She was light on her feet for a big woman, and when Lester dodged she turned back quick as a turkey hen. The pack of boys was in the way, so Lester couldn't run on past the porch steps; without intending to, they headed him, and Aunt Belle and Uncle O.R. drove him up onto the porch and through the front door. The women had all come out of the kitchen into the hall, and Uncle George Washington and Uncle Will were starting out of the living room. Lester took the only open route—up the stairs.

Aunt Belle had cut in ahead of Uncle O.R., and she started up, too. She had her skirts bundled in front of her like a load of laundry, and she was going as fast as Lester.

He got to the top of the stairs and ran into the room over the living room, flinging the door to behind him. But Aunt Belle was right there and caught it before it slammed. When Aunt Belle and Uncle O.R. and the rest of the boys went into the room there was nobody in sight, but they could hear the sound of breathing under the bed. And through the cracks between the floorboards they could hear Uncle Fowler snoring by the fire down in the living room.

Aunt Belle got down on her hands and knees and looked under.

"Uh *huh*!" she said. "Young mister, I been a-laying for you."

She crawled partway under, caught Lester by the foot, and dragged him out spread-eagled, turning over a chamber pot that had been left unemptied under the edge of the bed.

The boys got downstairs again in time to see the golden shower spend its last drops upon the head and shoulders of Old Ant'ny, who sat unmoving as before, looking straight ahead, as though he had foreseen it all years ago and was resigned.

"Lor-dee!" Uncle O.R. said.

It was getting dark now. There was a lamp burning in the room, and you could no longer see out the windows. There was a moment that seemed to be the moment before anything else could happen.

And then Old Ant'ny's hat brim jerked upward just a fraction of an inch. "Maw, turn back the bed. These folks want to be gettin' on home."

Little snorts of laughter had been leaking out of Tol for some time, and now he let himself laugh. It was a good laugh, broad and free and loud, including all of us as generously as the shade we sat in, and not only those of us who were living, but Old Ant'ny and Maw Proudfoot and Uncle O.R. and Uncle Fowler and Aunt Belle and Lester and the rest whose bodies lay in their darkness nearby.

And I will never forget the ones who were still alive that day and how they looked: Old Tol with his hands at rest in his lap, laughing until tears ran down his face, and the others around him laughing with him. It was Tol's benediction, as I grew to know, on that expectancy of good and surprising things that had kept Lester's eyes, and Tol's, too, wide open for so long.

And years later my grandmother would tell me that down among the women, hearing Tol laugh, Miss Minnie had smiled the prim, matronly smile with which she delighted in him. "Mr. Proudfoot," she said. "Mr. Proudfoot is amused."

Part II

7 *Watch with Me*

(1916)

One of the vital organs of Ptolemy Proudfoot's farm was a small square building called simply "the shop." Here Tol worked, according to necessity, as a blacksmith, farrier, carpenter, and mender of harness and shoes. The shop contained a forge with a cranking bellows and an anvil resting on an oak block. A workbench, with a stout vise attached, ran along one wall under three small windows. Tools and spare parts and usable scraps lay on the bench or stood propped in corners or hung from nails. On good days when they could be left open, large double doors at the front end admitted a fine flow of light.

On days when the weather prevented work outdoors, Tol would go to the shop and putter, or he would go there and sit and think. But he puttered and thought to advantage, for he earned more than he spent and sold more than he bought. He would be in the shop in the fall and winter more than in the spring and summer. In the spring and summer it was a good place to set a hen,

and a couple of boxes for that purpose were fastened to
the wall at the end of the workbench nearest the front
doors.

Tol and his wife, Miss Minnie, and their neighbors
killed hogs as soon as the nights became dependably cold
in the fall. They wintered on backbone and spareribs and
sausage and souse, with a shoulder or ham now and then.
By spring they would begin to be a little tired of pork;
fried chicken began to be easy to imagine. That was when
Miss Minnie would begin to save eggs and watch for her
hens to start setting. She liked to put several hens on
eggs, in the henhouse and in the shop, just as soon as
the weather began to warm up.

On the morning when this story begins, the chickens of that year were nearly all hatched. There was only
one red hen still hovering sixteen eggs in one of the boxes
in the shop. It was a fine morning early in August, dewy
and bright; the Katy's Branch valley was still covered
with a shining cloud of fog. It was 1916 and a new kind
of world was in the making on the battlefields of France,
but you could not have told it, standing on Cotman Ridge
with that dazzling cloud lying over Goforth in the valley,
and the woods and the ridgetops looking as clear and
clean as Resurrection Morning. Birds were singing. And
Tol could hear roosters crowing, it seemed to him, all
the way to Port William.

He had just stepped out after breakfast. It was later
than usual, because the day had begun crosswise. When

he had called his milk cows, they had not come. He had walked in the weak dawn-light down into the woods along the branch, where he found a water gap torn out by a recent freshet. From there he tracked the three cows down the wooded slopes halfway to Goforth before he found them and started them home. He drove them through the rent in the fence, wired it back with his hands well enough to hold until he could return with proper tools and more wire, and went on up the hill to chain them in their places in the barn.

And then when he was milking the third cow—a light-colored Jersey by the name of Blanche of whom he was particularly fond—she solemnly raised her right hind foot, plastered with manure, and set it down again in the half-filled bucket of milk.

Though he was a large, physically exuberant man who had been a wrestler famous all the way to Hargrave in his younger days, Tol was not a man of violence. But once he got Blanche's foot out of the bucket, he had to sit there on his stool a good while before he could rid himself of the thought of joyful revenge. On the one hand, he sympathized with the cow. He thought he knew how she felt. It would be exasperating, after finding a hole in the fence and escaping into the wide world, to be driven home again, chained to a stanchion, and required to yield one's milk into a bucket. On the other hand, Tol's sense of justice was outraged. He had raised the cow lovingly from a calf; he had sheltered and fed

135

and doctored her; he had loved and petted and pampered her—and now just look how she had treated him! He leaned his head back into her flank and began to milk again.

"Blanche," he said, "I ought to knock you in the head." He milked on in silence, his anger ebbing away. "But I don't reckon I will."

He stripped her dry, poured the bucket of ruined milk into the hog trough, turned the cows back into the pasture, and went to the house for breakfast, carrying one empty milk bucket and one full one.

"Did you have trouble with the cows?" Miss Minnie asked. She set Tol's breakfast before him and started straining the milk.

Tol told her.

"Why, the old hussy!" Miss Minnie said. "I'll bet you wanted to knock her in the head. Did you?"

"Not this time," Tol said. And that made him laugh, for he thought he was at the end of the story, but he was not at the end of it yet.

The day had begun so contrarily that when Tol went by the shop to see about the setting hen on his way to the barn, he was not much surprised to hear her squawking in extreme dismay before he opened the door. When he opened the door he saw what the fuss was about.

A big snake had climbed the locust tree next to the shop, crawled out along a limb and under the eave of the building, and was now descending along a crossbrace toward the hen's nest. The snake was the kind known as a cowsucker, and it was big enough to swallow every egg in the nest. Tol was not particularly afraid of snakes, though he preferred not to walk up on one by surprise, nor did he hate them. He rather liked to have them around to catch mice, and now and then he would capture one to put in his corncrib. All the same, he did not welcome them into his hens' nests.

"You got to change your mind, boy," he said to the snake, who was now looking at him with its head erect, flickering its tongue. "You going to have to take your business elsewhere."

Tol thought at first that he would just catch the snake by the end of the tail and buy its goodwill by letting it catch mice a while in the corncrib. But a cowsucker is a grouchy kind of snake, much inclined to stand on its rights, and when Tol reached out for its tail, the snake contracted into loops and threatened to bite Tol's hand. There is no danger of being poisoned by a cowsucker's bite, but when one threatens to bite you, you are very much inclined to draw back in a hurry whatever you have stuck out, and you are inclined to take the gesture as an insult.

Tol was a man slow to anger, but when the snake

made as if to strike his hand, his mental state reverted to the moment, by no means long enough ago, when the cow had put her foot in the bucket.

"Well," he said to the snake, "if you don't need killing, then Hell ain't hot."

Tol was thoroughly mad by then, and also anxious for the hen and her nest of eggs. On her account, he wanted to get rid of the snake with the least possible commotion and in the biggest possible hurry.

So he ran back to the house and put a shell into the chamber of the old ten-gauge shotgun that he had inherited from his father. It was a hard-shooting, single-barreled weapon that Tol's father had called Old Fetcher, "for it was a sure way to send for fresh meat."

When he got back to the shop, Tol flung the door open for light, stood back so as to minimize disturbance to the hen, leveled the long, rusty barrel point-blank at the snake's head, and fired—only to see the snake, with maddening dignity and aplomb, slowly depart by way of the hole that Old Fetcher had blasted through the wall.

Tol fully appreciated how funny that was, but he had no trouble in postponing his laughter. The hen, for one thing, was off the nest now and raising Cain, as if Tol and not the snake were the chief threat to her peace of mind.

"Get back on that nest and shut up," Tol said.

He picked up a stick and ran around to the side of

the building, but the snake, after the manner of its kind, was nowhere to be seen. And so Tol patched the hole he had made in the wall, and chinked up the place under the eave where he thought the snake had come in. He shooed the offended hen back into the shop and shut the door.

"Be quiet, now," he said. "You're going to live."

He went back to the house, got another shell for the gun, reloaded it, and propped it against the shop door. If that snake showed itself again, it was going to become an ex-criminal in a hurry.

Tol went to the garden then, unhooked his hoe from the fence, sharpened it, and began cleaning out a row of late cabbages.

Steady work quiets the mind. Tol began to feel that he had got the day off to a straight start at last. He had nearly finished the cabbage row when he saw Sam Hanks's truck come in and stop in front of the barn.

Sam got out and came strolling into the garden. He wanted to borrow Tol's posthole-digging tools so he could set a clothesline post for his mother.

Sam was Miss Minnie's favorite nephew, the only son of her only sister and Warren Hanks, a hardworking but somehow luckless tenant farmer. Sam had not followed in his father's footsteps. "He loves a damned wheel," his father had said, and Sam earned a modest living for himself and his now-widowed mother by hauling livestock and other things in his truck. He owned plenty of mechanic's tools, but when he needed something to dig with, he came to Tol.

For that matter, Sam was apt to show up at Tol's and Miss Minnie's pretty often, even when he didn't want to borrow something. He returned his aunt's affection, and he liked Tol. Moreover, he enjoyed Tol. When Sam came walking into the garden that morning, Tol looked completely in character. He stood amid the rows of his garden, which he kept with an almost perfect attention to detail. And in the midst of that neatness and order, Tol could have been a scarecrow, albeit an unusually big one. He wore an utterly shapeless old straw hat. And he had now been long enough beyond the reach and influence of Miss Minnie that part of his shirttail was out, one of his cuffs was unbuttoned, and his left shoe was untied. Tol's clothes always looked as if they were making a strenuous and perhaps hopeless effort just to stay somewhere in his vicinity.

"Well," Sam Hanks said to him, "looks like I been elected to put up a clothesline. Don't reckon I could borrow your diggers and all."

"Why, sure," Tol said. "They're yonder in the shop. Watch, now, when you go in and don't get snakebit."

Tol then told Sam what had happened. But he just said he had let the snake get away from him; he didn't tell about shooting the hole in the wall. He wanted to save that for when he could laugh about it. He was a man who had been mistreated by a cow and a snake all in the same morning, and he felt sore and aggrieved.

But while he was still commenting to Sam on the cowsucker's extreme ill humor, he saw his neighbor, Thacker Hample, coming over the ridge, and then another trouble returned to his mind.

*T*hacker Hample belonged to a large family locally noted for the fact that from one generation to another not a one of them had worked quite right. Their commonest flaw was poor vision. When he could find them or somebody found them for him, Thacker wore glasses with lenses as thick as shoe soles. Walter Cotman said that if Nightlife's nose had been a quarter of an inch longer, he would have been illiterate—but that was Walter Cotman. They called Thacker Nightlife on the theory that he could not tell daylight from dark, and therefore was liable to conduct his nightlife in the daytime. The name had a certain sexual glamour that appealed to Thacker Hample himself. When he had occasion to call himself by name, he usually called himself Nightlife— though he didn't ordinarily say much of anything to anybody.

But Nightlife was incomplete, too, in some other way. There were times when spells came on him, when he would be sad and angry and confused and maybe dangerous, and nobody could help him. And sometimes he would have to be sent away to the asylum where, Uncle Otha Dagget said, they would file him down and reset his teeth.

When he was quiet, he was quieter than anybody, and Nightlife had been quiet for a long time. But then the week came for the annual revival at Goforth Church, and unbeknownst to anybody but himself Nightlife decided that on the third night he himself would be the preacher, and he spent most of the preceding night getting ready. He made up a sermon and a prayer or two, and picked out some appropriate hymns. And on the night before Tol's trouble with the cow and the snake, Nightlife presented himself to the regular preacher and the visiting preacher and told them that he was going to preach the evening's sermon. In his sermon, as Tol and the others would understand later, Nightlife wanted to tell what it was like to be himself. That was what he knew, and what he had to say. It had to come out because at that time anyhow, it was all he had in him.

It would have been better if the two preachers had just said all right. But they, who well knew that they knew neither the day nor the hour of the coming of the Son of man, were in fact not prepared for anything unscheduled. They told Nightlife that the evening's service would have to proceed as planned. And that was when Nightlife's time of quietness came to an end and, as the eyewitnesses all agreed, he throwed a reg'lar fit.

He flung his Bible down at the feet of the horrified young preachers. He threw his arms wide apart, laughed a loud contemptuous laugh, and asked them whose church they thought it was. They thought it was their church, he said, but he reckoned they just might be a little bit mistaken: it was Jesus's church. And when Jesus came back, He would fork the likes of them into Hell as quick as look at them, and he, Nightlife, would at that time enjoy hearing them sing a different tune. He laughed again and bestowed upon them several epithets not normally used in church.

And so that evening's service did not, after all, proceed as planned. By a sort of general and unspoken deference, Tol Proudfoot, who was certainly the biggest of them and was probably the kindest, was elected to deal with Nightlife Hample. While the others stood around and listened and then, tiring, began to drift away, Tol talked to Nightlife, whose anger had begun to subside into confusions of sorrow, regret, and self-pity. No clever persuasion was involved. With his big hand resting on Nightlife's shoulder or his knee, Tol told him that everybody liked him and didn't hold anything against him and thought he was a good fellow and wanted him to go home now and get a good night's sleep. Tol told him all that over and over again, and finally Nightlife allowed his old mother to lead him home.

———

But nobody, least of all Tol, thought it would end there. Tol figured that having dealt with Nightlife once, he would have to deal with him again. And so when he saw Nightlife flinging himself over the ridgetop and down toward the barn, he wasn't surprised, though he certainly was sorry.

"Trouble comes in bunches," he said to Sam.

From where Nightlife came over the ridge, he could look right into Tol's garden, and he had on his glasses. That he saw Tol and Sam was obvious enough to them; he even seemed to have the idea of coming directly to where they were. But then when he crossed the road and entered Tol's driveway, Nightlife appeared to lose his intention; perhaps he had wanted to talk with Tol alone, and Sam's presence put him off. He wandered past the house into the barn lot. Now he was pretending, perhaps, that he did not know they were there and that he was just looking around to see if Tol was at home.

"You looking for me?" Tol called. "Here I am."

Nightlife then started toward the garden gate, went past the shop, saw Tol's old shotgun leaning there, and picked it up. He opened the breech to see if it was loaded. When he closed the breech again they could hear the snap of the lock all the way up there in the garden. Nightlife balanced the gun in his hands for a moment as if he were thinking of buying it. And then he laid it over his shoulder and turned away.

"Uh-oh," Tol said. He started toward the gate with

Sam Hanks stepping between the same pair of rows behind him.

"Don't take my gun, Nightlife!" Tol called, trying to sound not too much concerned, and yet unable to keep the tone of pleading entirely out of his voice. "I'm liable to need it!"

Tol had started to hurry. He hung his hoe on the fence by the gate and went on toward the shop.

Nightlife was hesitating. He turned back toward the door of the shop, as though he might actually put the gun back where he got it.

But then he turned away again. He said, not to Tol and Sam, rather to himself, but in too loud a voice, as if he did not quite expect himself to be able to hear, "Why, a damned fellow just as well shoot hisself, I reckon."

"Wait, Nightlife!" Tol said. And then he added an endearment, as he usually did, to soften what might have seemed a reprimand: "Hold on, sweetheart."

But Nightlife was already starting down through the pasture toward the woods with the gun on his shoulder.

"I expect I'll just ease along with him a ways," Tol said to Sam. "You go tell Miss Minnie, and then drive over and tell Walter Cotman and Tom and Braymer. Or send word to them if they're out at work. And then you come with us."

Tol was watching Nightlife while he talked to Sam.

"Mind that old gun, now. If he's crazy enough to shoot hisself, he might be crazy enough to shoot you."

"Or you," Sam said.

"Or me," Tol said. He stepped off down the slope, following the dark path Nightlife had made in the chewy grass.

When he heard the screen door slam as Sam stepped into the kitchen, a kind of wonder came over Tol, for almost in the twinkling of an eye he had crossed the boundary between two worlds. In spite of the several small troubles of that morning, he had been in a world that was more or less the world he thought it was, and where at least some things happened more or less as he intended. But now he was walking down through the wet grass of his cow pasture toward the edge of his woods, a place as familiar to him as the palm of his own hand, in a world and a day in which he intended nothing and foresaw nothing.

He hurried a little, not to catch up with Nightlife, but to keep him in sight, which would be harder to do once they were in the woods. And it was into the woods that Nightlife was going. He was not going in a hurry, but he was not loitering either. He walked like a man with a destination—though where, in that direction, he could be going was a mystery to Tol.

And then Nightlife took the gun from his shoulder, placed it in the crook of his right arm, and went in

among the young cedars that bordered the woods' edge
at that place. He disappeared as completely as if he had
suddenly dived into water, but with less commotion.
Not a bush trembled after he disappeared, and Tol feared
that he would lose him. He went in himself at the same
place, and for a while, among the cedars and other young
low-branching trees, he could not see six feet ahead. And
then, not far from the edge, the woods became taller and
more open, and Tol could see Nightlife again.

He was no longer going so directly down the slope,
but was slanting to his right as though he intended to
go toward the river along that side of the Katy's Branch
valley, and soon, when he was well into the woods, he
again altered his course so that he was not going downhill
at all, but was going along the level contour of the slope.
He was not walking fast, nor did he appear to be looking
at anything. He seemed totally preoccupied, as though
all his attention were demanded by whatever was in his
mind.

Tol had thought of calling out to Nightlife, but
had rejected the thought. The presence of Old Fetcher
made it hard to know what to say. Tol had known Nightlife as long as Nightlife had been in this world to be
known, but when one of his spells was on him, Nightlife
was a stranger to everybody. There was no telling, then,
what he might or might not do. Tol didn't want to cause
him to shoot himself in order to win an argument about

whether or not he was going to shoot himself. Nor was Tol on his own account at all eager to face the business end of Old Fetcher.

He decided just to follow along, keeping Nightlife in sight as best he could. He would not try to catch up; he would try not to fall too far behind; he would say nothing. And Tol's decision then established what he and the others would do the rest of that day and into the next. They would let whatever it was run its course, if it would. They would stop Nightlife from using the gun, if they had to and if they were able. At every considerable change of direction, Tol broke a branch end and left it dangling as a mark for Sam. Otherwise, the passage of two men over the dead leaves of the woods' floor ought to be legible enough.

Nightlife and his widowed mother lived on a farm of maybe fifty acres that lay back in one of the several hollows that drained into Katy's Branch. The farm was mostly hillside. It contained no ridgeland at all, and no bottomland except for a narrow shelf along the branch where the Hamples had their garden and where they had built a small log barn with a corncrib beside it. The house, built of logs like the barn, stood on the slope above the scrap of bottom, with privy and henhouse and smokehouse behind it. So far as the neighborhood remembered, nobody but Hamples had ever lived there.

The farm was a remnant of land that had been overlooked or left out of the surveys of the larger boundaries that once surrounded it, or it had been sold off one of the larger boundaries at some time during the frenzy of settlement and speculation that accompanied the white people's first taking of the land.

There had been a time—way back when the trees of the original forest were yet growing on it—when the place was fertile. But the first-comers, having no other land to farm, cut the trees from the slopes, patch by patch, growing little crops of tobacco and corn until fertility declined by the combined action of plow and rain, and then abandoning the land again to bushes and then trees, only to repeat the whole process in forty or fifty years. In the early days, perhaps, the Hamples lived up to the standard of most of their neighbors. They had the produce of what was still a productive little farm. They had what they could kill or pick or dig up in the stands of virgin forest that still stood all around. Some of the Hample men rode flatboats or log rafts down the spring tides to New Orleans, for among the prized possessions of their descendants were a few Spanish and French coins that had been carried back on the overland trails.

But as the forests were cut down and the wild bounty of the country diminished and the soil of the slopes fled away beneath the axes and jumper plows of generation after generation of Hamples, the family's life became ever more marginal. They kept a milk cow or two, a team of mules, meat hogs, and poultry. They raised a patch of corn and a little shirttail crop of tobacco. They kept the garden. They hunted and fished and trapped, dug roots and stripped bark, gathered the wild potherbs and fruit. From the corn that they and their animals did not eat, they distilled a palatable and potent whiskey, of which they sold as much as they did not drink. And yet their life declined until they were reduced to dependence on daywork for their neighbors, who did not need much help. And yet the Hamples persevered, and even provided a sort of hearty and bitter amusement to themselves. Delbert, Nightlife's father, as an old man became famous for his boast, often repeated in the store at Goforth or in the bank at Port William: "I started out with damn near nothing, and I have multiplied it by hard work until I am going to end up with damn near what I started out with."

But the Hamples were known, too, for their handiness. The neighborhood liked to boast of them that they could "make anything or fix anything." They seemed to be born, virtually every one of them, with an uncanny mastery of tools and materials. When weak vision got bred into the line—which it did fairly early—it apparently made little difference, for Hample hands were so adept that they seemed to possess a second sight in their very fingertips. As industrial farm machinery entered the country and became more complicated, the Hamples in a way came into their own. None of them ever had the enterprise to open a proper shop, but their neighbors were forever bringing them something to fix.

Large families of Hamples had been raised in their snug hollow with its two slopes facing one another across the rocky notch of the branch, for the Hample men, whatever the condition of their fields, were fertile, and they married fertile women. As soon as they got big enough to leave or to marry, the Hample generations scattered like seeds from an opened pod. Always, until now, somebody would be left to start the cycle again. But after his father died, Nightlife stayed at home with his mother; he did not marry, and nobody thought he ever would. Even as a Hample, Nightlife was an oddity, and nobody could quite account for him. He had inherited the mechanical gifts of the Hamples; people said that he could do anything with his hands. And yet he seemed also to have been endowed with an ineptitude that was all his own. For instance, when he was about ten years old he contrived a jew's harp out of an old clock spring and a piece of walnut; it was a marvel of cunning artistry, as everybody affirmed, but when he attempted to play it, it very nearly cut off his tongue. He was a Hample, plain enough, but it was as though when he was a baby his mechanically minded siblings had taken him apart and lost some of the pieces, which they then replaced with just whatever they found lying around. Nightlife lacked almost entirely the rough sense of humor that had accompanied other Hamples into and out of this world. And in addition to the capability of becoming drunk, which all Hample men before him had had in varying degrees, Nightlife had the capability of becoming crazy. His mind, which contained the lighted countryside of Katy's Branch and Cotman Ridge, had a leak in it somewhere, some little hole through which now and again would pour the whole darkness of the darkest night—so that instead of walking in the country he knew and among his kinfolks and neighbors, he would be afoot in a limitless and undivided universe, completely dark, inhabited only by himself. From there he would want to call out for rescue, and that was when nobody could tell what he was going to do next, and perhaps he could not tell either.

Or that was what it looked like to Tol, who had thought much about it. And that was what Nightlife himself looked like that morning when Tol followed him down into the woods—he looked like somebody who didn't know where in all the world he was, who didn't know anybody else was there to see him, much less follow along after him.

Tol followed him nevertheless, and yet he did so with a sense of foregone conclusion. He had too much courtesy, if he had not had too much sense, to believe for sure that Nightlife would die by his own hand that day, or even soon, if ever. But he believed that he would die somehow sometime, and that when he did die, the name and the prospects of the Hamples would depart forever from what until then would be known as the Hample Place.

*I*n assuming that the history and the future of the Hamples in their native hollow would end with Night-life, Tol was right. Fifty years later, on a Sunday ramble with Elton Penn and the Rowanberry brothers and Burley Coulter, I walked up the branch through what once had been the Hample Place. It was early April. The spring work had started. When Elton and I drove down to the Rowanberry Place after dinner that day, the Rowanberrys said they were stiff and sore and needed to walk. So we climbed up through the woods onto the Coulter Ridge where we ran into Burley, who had nothing better to do, he said, than to go with us. There were five of us then, not hurrying or going anyplace in particular; we were just walking along and looking at the season and the weather, talking of whatever the places we came to reminded us of.

We walked down the hollow the Coulters call Step-stone, past the old barn that stands there, and on down to the Katy's Branch road. We followed the road up Katy's Branch a little beyond Goforth, and then we crossed the branch and went up into the woods along the hollow that divided the Hample Place. By then the Hample Place, the Tol Proudfoot Place, the Cotman Place, and others had all been dissolved into one large property that belonged to a Louisville doctor, who had bought it for a weekend retreat and then lost interest in it. Now, except for the best of the ridges, which were rented and farmed badly, the land was neither farmed nor lived on. Every building on it was ruining or already ruined, and the good hillside pastures were covered with young trees—which Burley Coulter said was all right with him.

"It's a damned shame, anyhow," said Elton, who did not want to forgive the neglect.

"Well, a fellow looking for something better, he don't want to stay in a place like this," Art Rowanberry said.

"Was that doctor looking for something better when he bought it?" Mart said.

"I reckon he thought he already had something better."

"Well," Mart said, laughing a little to refuse the argument with his brother, "anyhow, I reckon the more trees, the more coons."

They were all hunters. All the country around us was thickly crisscrossed with the nighttime passages of their hunts. They had worked over it, too, and as boys had played over it. They knew it by day and by night, and knew something about every scrap of it. As we came up by Goforth Church, the long-abandoned store building, and the site of the vanished schoolhouse, and then passed the Goforth Hill road that went up alongside the

Proudfoot Place, they began to tell stories about Tol Proudfoot, quoting the things he had said that nobody who had known him ever forgot. And then when we started up along the Hample branch, they told about the time Nightlife threw his fit, and about Tol and the others following him through the woods.

"What kind of farmers were the Hamples?" I asked.

And Art Rowanberry said, "Oh, they growed a very good *winter* crop."

The Hample Place, when we got to it, no longer looked like anybody's place. The woods, which had started to return after Delbert Hample's death, had now completely overgrown it. The young trees had grown big enough to have begun to shade out the undergrowth. The barn and other outbuildings were gone without a trace. The house had slowly weathered away beneath its tin roof, which with its gables intact had sunk down onto the collapsed walls. Only the rock chimney stood, its corners still as straight as on the day they were laid. We peered under one of the fallen gables and looked straight into a buzzard's nest containing one fuzzy white chick and one unhatched egg.

We had come as far as we wanted to go, and we rested there a while before we started back. It was a pleasant place, sheltered, opening to the west, so that the sun would have warmed it on winter afternoons. The north slope above the house would have been good land once, and now with the woods thriving on it again, you

155

could imagine how it once might have evoked a vision of home in whatever landless, wandering Hample had first come—though his and his descendants' attempt to farm there could only have proved it no place to farm. Their way of farming, in fact, had destroyed maybe forever the possibility of farming there. And so you felt that the trees had returned as a kind of justice. They had only drawn back and paused a moment while a futile human experiment had been tried and suffered in that place, and had failed at last as it was bound to do.

As we were leaving, we wandered past the fallen house and across the old garden spot to the branch. And then we saw that the chimney was not the only thing left standing, for there in the middle of the streambed stood a cylinder of laid rock that once had lined the Hamples' well, and now it stood free like another chimney, turned wrong side out, where the stream had cut the earth from around it.

And so the Hamples had come and gone and left their ruin. And now the trees had returned. The trees on the little shelf where the garden had been were tall young tulip poplars that lifted their opening buds into the still light and air of that evening with such an unassuming calm that you could almost believe they had been there always.

Art Rowanberry, I remember, stood looking at them a long time. And then, turning to go, he said,

"Well, old Nightlife didn't have to leave this world for want of wood, I don't reckon."

Tol had just begun to wonder when Sam was going to show up when Sam showed up. Tol raised his hand to him, and Sam nodded. In silence then they picked their way along together, Sam walking behind Tol. Between themselves and Nightlife, they kept a sort of room of visibility, the size of which varied according to the density of the foliage. They meant to stay separate from Nightlife by the full breadth of that room. When the foliage thickened, they drew closer to Nightlife to keep him in sight. Where the trees were old and there was not much underbrush, they slowed down and let him get farther ahead.

After a while Nightlife came to a pile of rocks that had been carried from some long-abandoned corn or tobacco patch, and he sat down, laying the gun across his lap. He appeared now to be carrying the gun as if it were some mere hand tool, not recognizing what it was, just as he appeared to grant no recognition to himself or to where he was. When he stopped and sat down, Tol and Sam stood still. When he got up and started on again, they followed.

After a while Braymer Hardy was there behind Sam. And not long after that, when Tol again looked back,

Walter Cotman and Tom Hardy were there. Tol stopped
them then, and beckoned them close. He was older than
the oldest of them by twenty years; he could have been
father to them all, and they came obediently into whispering distance.

"Boys," he said, "ain't no use in us walking lined
up so that old gun could hit us all with one shot. Kind
of fan out. We'll keep him in sight better that way."

They fanned out as he said. And now the room of
sight that had been defined only by a diameter was given
a circumference as well. As they moved along, they continued to draw closer together or move farther apart,
according to visibility. In that moving room that at once
divided and held them together the only clarity was their
intent not to let Nightlife be further divided from them.

They moved along with him wherever he moved.
And he went, still, pretty much level along the face of
the slope, into the draws and out around the points
through old woods and through thicket, across pastures
and tobacco patches, but mostly in the woods. Sometimes
he would stop or sit down, and then they would wait,
and when he went ahead they would go with him. That
Nightlife was not himself, that he had become merely
the vehicle of something he suffered that they had not
suffered, they could tell by the way he moved and carried
himself, the way he looked always straight ahead and
always at the ground. He moved like a man in the con-

centration of urgent bodily pain, though they knew his pain was not of the body. Maybe he was not going to kill himself, they thought. Maybe he just needed something he did not have, had never had, did not know how to ask for, maybe did not know the name of. But they knew also that Old Fetcher was an influential weapon. It was not a squirrel rifle—not a gun with which you could confidently undertake to shoot yourself just a little. If you picked up Old Fetcher, declaring that you might as well shoot yourself, then they knew as surely as if they held it in their own hands, you couldn't put that gun down again without deciding *not* to shoot yourself.

It was a long time since morning now, and the day was getting hot. In the woods it was still and close. All five of them had sweated through their shirts. And still they moved along with Nightlife, and still they formed their rough and ever-shifting semicircle at the limit of sight. They were squirrel hunters and they knew how to move unobtrusively and quietly in the woods. In the spell of Nightlife's silence and their own, strangeness came over them, as if they had died and come back in another time. Everything familiar had become strange. What they saw around them now seemed no longer to be what they knew and had always known, but seemed only to remind them of a time when they had known those things. They were following a man whom it had never occurred to them to follow before, who now had become central to their lives, and who perhaps was trying to find his way out of this world.

*B*y noon they had come all the way down the Katy's Branch valley and turned into the valley of the river, still keeping along the mostly wooded face of the bluff, high up. Now they were conscious of the bigger space and larger light; down through openings among the treetops they could see the river itself bending across the valley floor between its two parallel rows of trees, leaving the wide bottomlands first on one side and then the other. They could see the cornfields and houses and farm buildings in the bottoms on down into the blue distance halfway to Hargrave. Off somewhere on the far side of the river they heard a dinner bell.

And now they were aware also of the world going on, unaware of them and their extraordinary worry and purpose. It seemed unaccountable to them that they should know so well where they were when nobody else in all the world had any idea.

Presently they came to a deep crease in the face of the slope, worn there over the millennia by a steep wet-weather stream known as Squire's Branch. And here instead of turning into the hollow in order to keep on the level as he had been doing, Nightlife slanted down into the dry bed of the branch and then turned straight down toward the river, stair-stepping down the tumbled rocks of the streambed. The others followed in their half-circle, with Tol in the center and the others fanned out on either side.

They stayed in the wooded hollow, but as the slopes gentled they could see open pasture off through the trees first on the left and then also on the right. And then they could see a little tobacco patch on the left. From time to time, the foliage opening, they could see the little store at Squire's Landing and the house on the slope above it where Uncle Otha and Aunt Cordie Dagget lived and farmed a little and fished a little and kept the store and the landing and kept an eye on the comings and goings of the neighborhood.

When Uncle Otha and Aunt Cordie's house came full into sight, Nightlife climbed out of the streambed onto the open slope. And then he walked down across Uncle Otha's cow pasture, through the yard gate, across the yard, up onto the back porch, and through the kitchen door without so much as a knock.

Tol stopped at the edge of the woods and the others came up beside him.

"What now?" Walter Cotman said.

Tol uttered a sound that was partly a laugh and partly a grunt. What he should have done was all too clear to him now, and to the rest of them, too. He should have sent Sam Hanks and Tom Hardy, who were on that side of the branch, to Uncle Otha's ahead of Nightlife. But it had not occurred to him that Nightlife, who earlier

had avoided him and Sam and who had spent the whole
morning skulking along in the woods by himself, would
think of going right into somebody's house. Tol had his
lower lip between his teeth.

"Well, what are we going to do?" Braymer Hardy
said.

"Boy, there ain't nothing *to* do. We can't go barging
into Aunt Cordie's kitchen ourselves. He's the only one
that's got a gun. And if we had guns they wouldn't do
us any good, unless we wanted to shoot somebody or get
shot, which I reckon we don't."

"So I reckon we're going to wait," Walter Cotman
said. And he sat down.

The others seemed to consider sitting down also for
they would not have minded a rest, but nobody but
Walter did so. Nor could they stay where they were.
Watching the house always, they eased gradually down
into the yard. They did not go closer to the house than
the yard gate for fear of inciting Nightlife to some damage
they feared without naming. The worst they could imagine now had as good a license to happen as the best, and
there was nothing at the moment that they could do.
They did not go to the shade for the same reason that
they did not sit down: it would not have been right. All
the morning, it seemed to them, they had been walking
the rim of the world, a narrow, shadowy, steeply sloping
margin between life and death, and this imposed a strict
propriety on them all. But from where they stood even

with the kitchen windows open, they could not tell what was happening inside.

*T*hey weren't going to know what was happening inside until after the story was over and Uncle Otha told Sam Hanks and Sam told Tol and Tol told the others at church on Sunday morning.

What happened was that Uncle Otha and Aunt Cordie were eating dinner. It was fried catfish. The others knew that much; they could smell it out in the yard. It smelled better than they wanted it to, for they were hungry themselves by then.

"Do you want some cornbread, Othy?" Aunt Cordie said.

And then the screen door opened and here came Nightlife right into the kitchen with that old gun cradled in the crook of his left arm and looking like he was trying hard to remember something that he only barely remembered forgetting. They had not heard him until he put hand to the door and the spring sang.

He seemed to get clear into the middle of the kitchen before he realized that he was among people.

When he saw Uncle Otha and Aunt Cordie sitting at the table, looking at him, their laden forks suspended between their plates and their mouths, he said, "Let us earnestly compose our hearts for prayer."

"Son," Uncle Otha said to Sam Hanks, "I did earnestly compose my heart for prayer. I was afraid if I looked up I'd find my head in my plate."

When Uncle Otha and Aunt Cordie bowed their heads, Nightlife prayed. What he said Uncle Otha was unable to report to Sam, for he said his mind had been occupied with a few words in his own behalf.

It was, anyhow, a long prayer that Nightlife prayed; Uncle Otha ran out of anything to say in his own behalf before it was over, and under the circumstances he was unable to think of anything to say in anybody else's behalf. He and Aunt Cordie sat there with their heads down while that good fish got cold on the platter and Nightlife prayed, but not for them or at them; he prayed as if he were off somewhere by himself, and out loud but not too loud, Uncle Otha said, as if he suspected Old Marster was present but too deaf to overhear a thought or a whisper.

Aunt Cordie kept her head bowed to the end, for she would honor even a crazy man's prayer. But when Nightlife said, "Amen," she looked straight at him. "Thacker Hample, now what *is* all this foolishness? Sit down, child, and let me fix you a plate."

But Nightlife just stared at her and at Uncle Otha, too, as if they, who had known him all his life, were strangers. His face was covered by a sort of blur of incomprehension, as if he not only did not recognize them but had no idea where he was.

"Son," Uncle Otha said, "put down that dad-damned old gun, now, and get yourself something to eat."

"I can't eat of that river," Nightlife said, "for it's of the passing of the flesh. I don't know where it has come from nor where it's a-going."

"Son, that river has come from up and it's a-going down. Take a chair, and let the woman fix you a bite of fish."

Aunt Cordie, who had got up, said, "Yes!" and reached out toward Nightlife as if to take hold of his arm.

Nightlife shrank away from her hand like a half-wild colt, and went back out the kitchen door.

"I went to the kitchen door and watched him go," Uncle Otha told Sam, "and then I seen you all was following along after him. So I sat down again and told the woman to pass the cornbread, for I had to eat and I didn't have all day."

When they had come out of the shadowy woods, the whole hillside, buildings and trees and all, quaked in the still sunlight. Under the strong light, the maples in Uncle Otha's yard seemed bent in profound meditation on their shadows now drawn in at their feet. Standing together just inside the yard gate, Tol and the other three quaked, too, and sweated in the fierce, bright fall of the noon heat. Not a leaf stirred anywhere. They heard what they would later know was Nightlife's prayer—not the words, but just the rising and falling sound of it. And then, more briefly, they heard the voices of Aunt Cordie and Uncle Otha.

And then the screen door was flung open and Nightlife came out, letting the door clap to behind him. When he stepped off the porch, he looked straight at the little band of men standing inside the yard gate with no more sign of recognition than if they had been posts or trees or not there at all. He followed the path around the house and down past the little store that would be closed until Uncle Otha finished his dinner. He turned upriver along the road; beyond the wooden bridge over Squire's Branch, he crossed the narrow bottom to the river and turned upstream again at the top of the bank.

They were following him again, easing along behind him as before, keeping him in sight. If he knew he was thus accompanied, he gave no sign, and he did not look back. They walked nonetheless in fear that he would look back, would see and recognize them, and that the sight of them would cause him to do they did not know what. They were too busy, picking their way along and keeping him and each other in sight, to have time to think much about anything else, but they never ceased to be conscious of the gun, and of the immense difference it made. It was the wand that transformed them all. Without it, they would have been men merely walking on the world. Having it there before them in the hands of a man who might do with it they did not know what, they were men walking between this present world and the larger one that lies beyond it and contains it.

When they had passed the store they had seen Put Woolfork sitting in the shade under the porch roof, waiting for Uncle Otha to come down and open up for the afternoon. Put, as they knew, had a misery that wouldn't let him work much in hot weather, and so he would walk down to the landing in the afternoon to fill himself up with Uncle Otha's gossip and free advice. They had not passed near enough to him to speak, though Tol had raised his hand. Put did not raise his hand in reply, for he was too absorbed in watching them. They knew that they would be the first subject of conversation in the store that afternoon. They expected that as soon as Put was fully informed of the dinnertime events in the Daggets' kitchen, he would be along.

They were right. Now that Nightlife was walking along the river, he began to stop more often. The river seemed to have attracted his notice as nothing had since he had spied Old Fetcher leaning against Tol's shop door. As he went along now, he would pause to stand and look at the shady water beneath the overleaning trees. Or if he came to a stump or a drift log, he would sit down and look. And so it was no trouble for Put, once he had been informed, to catch up with them. Tol was soon aware that somebody was coming along behind them, and before he looked he knew who it was. Glancing back, he would see Put watching them from a weed patch or from behind a tree, his face sticking out, curious—in truth, fascinated—and yet afraid. He had come to observe and report.

Put was a man of about Tol's age, somewhere in his mid-forties, though his face showed not a wrinkle. He was round of eye and face and form, as tight-skinned and smooth as an apple. "Put" was a foreshortening of Pussel Gut, a name that had been conferred upon him on his first day in school. Put lived on a tiny farm where the Cotman Ridge road came down into the river bottom. He kept three or four cows, which his wife milked, and with the help of his wife and his neighbors, he grew a little crop. The misery that kept him from working much in hot weather also did not allow him to work much in cold weather or in wet weather, or ever to do any work for very long if it was very hard. Put walked with his knees bent and his posterior slightly lowered as if at any moment he might be called upon to squat, so that even walking on level ground, he gave the impression that he was going down a steep hill. It was not a good idea to ask him how he was, for he would tell you. Tol nevertheless always asked him how he was. Tol was as good a friend as Put had.

Still, it made him uneasy to have Put tagging along. Though he did not like to know it, and would never have said so, he knew that Put, beyond being useless, could be a burden. He knew also that unlike most of the neighborhood, who either tolerated Put or ignored him, Walter Cotman despised him. It had not been but a few days since Tol had heard Walter say in Put's presence—as if Put were not there or as if it did not matter if he was— that he was "as no-account as a shit-for-a-living damned old housecat." Walter was a good farmer and a good dependable young man, and yet Tol knew that Walter had an edge to him as hard, sharp, and forthright as a good saw. Walter was a fastidious, demanding man, who did good work himself, who had no patience with bad work, and who said exactly and without hesitation whatever he thought. Walter's tongue, as Tol often said to Miss Minnie, was connected directly to his mind.

Tol knew furthermore that when Walter laid one of those opinions of his in front of all the world, the Hardy brothers would laugh at it. The Hardys were stout, good-natured, smiling fellows, enough alike almost to be twins, except that Tom pitched and Braymer caught, and Braymer never owned anything he wouldn't trade and Tom never owned anything he would. They were half Proudfoot, the sons of Tol's sister, and Tol took much pleasure and pride in them. But they were young yet, too willing to laugh. So far as he could, Tol would go along with Put just as he would go along with Nightlife; he would do what he had to do, or what he could. If, after it was over, it made a good story, then he would tell it; if it was funny, he would laugh. But now was no time for laughter.

Nightlife had stopped again. He had come to one of the rare places where the bank slanted down gently almost to the water's edge. He sat down on the exposed roots of a big water maple that leaned out over the water; the gun lay across his lap and his hands rested on the gun. All the trees were big there, the riverbank was clear of brush, and Tol and the others had fallen a long way back. From his distance behind them, Put could no longer see Nightlife at all. Presently Tol saw Put break cover and start forward. Put was curious; he wanted to be where he could look at Nightlife. But Tol knew that he also had got lonesome and was longing for company and approval. Wanting no more commotion than necessary, Tol eased quietly back to forestall him.

"How're you, Put?" Tol said.

"Aw, Tol, I ain't no good," Put said. "I've had my misery a right smart lately. You know how this weather does me. How you, Tol?" he asked sympathetically, as if Tol suffered from the same misery.

"Fine," Tol said.

"Well, Uncle Othy was telling me about Nightlife and all. What do you reckon is going to happen? You reckon he's going to shoot hisself?"

They were talking under the white trunk of a large

sycamore, well out of sight of Nightlife, but Put was peering ahead, trying to see him; he had hardly looked at Tol. "Where's he at?"

"He's yonder," Tol said.

Now, having seen Tol move back, the others were coming, too.

Walter Cotman came up beside Tol just as Put said, "Well, I just thought you might need some help."

And Tol imagined Walter saying to Put—or to one of the others, for he would say it in front of Put but not to him, "If somebody's going to get shot, he'd like to be on hand to see it, long as it ain't much trouble." Tol could hear it as plainly as if Walter had said it, though so far Walter had said nothing.

"Honey," Tol said to Walter, "I expect one of us ought to keep an eye on Nightlife. We don't want him to go off without us."

Walter nodded and went back.

"Why, sure," Tol said to Put. "A fellow never knows when he'll need help."

After Nightlife got up from the roots of the maple and started on, it was a long time before he stopped again. He stayed near the river, avoiding the farmsteads, using farm roads or cow paths when he came to them and they were going in his direction; where there was no beaten way, he kept to his course anyhow. Briar patches he went around; other obstacles he climbed or went through apparently without granting them notice of their existence. He went through patches of nettles up to his waist. He went through brakes of horseweeds and fields of corn that were over his head. He was not hurrying, but neither did he alter his pace or stop. And Tol followed just as steadily behind him, with the young men spread out on either side of him as before and Put Woolfork coming along behind. The crops having been laid by, the six of them walked in a deserted country even there among the fields, and as they walked, the hot bright afternoon stood tall and still above them. Around them, in the heat, the low fields shimmered and swayed.

Tol was hungry. He had not forgotten the smell of fried fish wafting out from Aunt Cordie Dagget's kitchen. He was sorry he had not thought to leave Walter or Sam to wait for Uncle Otha to open the store and bring along maybe some cheese and some crackers, or maybe a few cans of sardines. He did not wish to indulge such thoughts, but they came to him uninvited, for he was a big man and he was used to three big meals a day.

But he was troubled also because he knew—he had known ever since that moment at the Daggets' when he had watched Nightlife walk unchecked and preceded by no warning through Aunt Cordie's kitchen door—that the day was beyond their control. The only man who had control was Nightlife, who did not know he had it. Their proven helplessness at the Daggets' forced Tol to ac-

knowledge that he could not foretell any of the bad out-
comes that might lie ahead or any outcome at all, for
that matter. Maybe, he thought, you could keep a crazy
man with a gun from shooting you or somebody else, if
you could guess correctly what he was going to do and
watch closely enough and keep far enough away. But how
in the world you could keep him from shooting himself
if he wanted to, unless you had a gun yourself and shot
him first, Tol could not imagine.

And so along with heat and hunger and the beginning of weariness, Tol's mind began to be afflicted by a
sense of the futility, even the foolishness, of what he and
the others were doing. For a while his thoughts lurched
here and there as if unable to accept that there was not
something better to do, or a better way to do what they
were doing, some reasonability or sense that could be
invited in. But he gave that up, as he gave up with the
same motion of his mind the hope of food or rest or
comfort.

It was not going to make sense, not yet, and maybe
not for a long time, if ever. And for a while, maybe a
longish while, there would not be food or rest or comfort
either. When they got to the end of the story, he reckoned, they would at least eat. He said to himself, "I
reckon it would be better not to have got involved." But
he knew even so that helpless or not, hopeless or not, he
would go along with Nightlife until whatever happened
that would allow him to cease to go along. And he knew

that Walter and Sam and the Hardys would keep going as long as he did, just as he knew that Put would not. He thought, "I reckon I am involved."

*T*hey had had a quick drink where a spring fed into Squire's Branch just above Uncle Otha's tobacco patch, and none since. Nightlife had not stopped to drink at all. Now they saw Nightlife veer away from the river toward an isolated barn where they knew there was a cistern. The cistern was in a small lot now in the shade at one of the barn's eastward corners. Keeping their distance, they watched Nightlife enter the lot, unhook a tin can from the barn wall, and pump himself a drink. He leaned the gun against the barn when he took down the can, and now he sat down on the cistern top with his back to the gun and with the full can of water in his hand.

"Lordy Lord," Tol thought, "if only one of these boys was close enough to snatch that old gun and run with it!"

But they were not close enough. They were standing in the sun at the edge of a cornfield, scattered out as before but—except for Put who had kept his distance from them as they from Nightlife—they were well within sight of one another, watching Nightlife who was sitting and resting in the shade with that can of cool water in his hand. With the cistern in sight, they suffered from their thirst. Nightlife took his time. The shade held him, and he sat there, sipping water from the can, while the barn swallows dipped and circled around him and over-head. And still he kept the same straight-ahead fixation on whatever was on his mind; he did not turn his head this way or that; he did not appear to be looking at anything.

After a while—an almost insufferable while for those who watched, thirsty, at the weedy edge of the cornfield, furnishing dinner to the sweatbees and the deerflies—he got up, hung the can back on its nail, picked up the gun, and went on in the same direction as before.

When Nightlife went out of sight into a wooded hollow, well beyond gun range of the barn, Tol's little company headed for the cistern—the Hardy brothers first, running, Sam Hanks not far behind them, and then Walter Cotman, who disdained to concede by any haste that he was as thirsty as the others, and then Tol. When Tol got almost to the little cistern lot, Put Woolfork emerged from the cornfield.

Now that they were close enough to one another, the Hardy brothers were almost as eager to talk as to drink.

"Whew!" Tom was saying as Tol came up. "When I seen him go in at Uncle Othy's, I didn't know what to expect."

He had pumped for Sam, and now he pumped again while Braymer held the can under the spout.

"I sure didn't want to hear that old gun go off," Braymer said. He grinned, shook his head, and wiped his mouth. "Uncle Tol," he said, "I don't reckon you was worried."

Tol laid his hat on the cistern top and wiped his face on his sleeve. "No," he said, "I wasn't worried. A man has a fit one night in church, and the next day picks up a loaded gun and goes off into the woods by hisself, and then walks in on an old couple at dinnertime without a knock or a 'come in,' that ain't no kind of a worry."

"What I want to know," Braymer said, having drunk and handed the can to his brother, "is how long can he keep up this traveling. Don't you reckon he'll get hungry before long? He ain't had no dinner."

"We ain't either," Sam said, "that I noticed."

"I reckon a man going to shoot hisself don't need to worry much about dinner," Tom said.

"How do you know he's going to shoot hisself?"

"Well, he said he was, didn't he?"

"He said he might as well. Maybe he ain't going to."

"Maybe he ain't."

Walter filled the can and offered it to Tol.

"Drink," Tol said.

Walter drank, refilled the can, and handed it to Tol.

"Well," Walter said, gazing off where Nightlife had disappeared, "if the damned fool is going to shoot hisself, why don't he go on and do it, and let the rest of us get back to work?"

That was Walter exactly, Tol thought. He would not leave a thought unsaid. And he could not ignore a difference.

But Walter did not leave, as Tol—and Walter himself—knew he would not. He said no more. He simply snorted, seeing that Put had now come up and seated himself on the cistern top.

Having emptied the can once fast and once more slowly, Tol handed it to Tom Hardy who was still at the pump, and stepped off toward the woods' edge, begrudging himself the three or four minutes he had stopped to drink.

Tol had not gone many steps from the barn before Sam Hanks put his hat back on and started after him. If there was danger in Nightlife, then Tol walked at risk now as he approached the woods; though Tol could not see Nightlife, Nightlife, if he wished, could see Tol. Once again it was possible for Sam to imagine the single abrupt syllable that was Old Fetcher's entire vocabulary. Sometimes during that day it had been possible to forget the old gun's plain and sudden eloquence; sometimes it had not been. Sam remembered it now with an exact presentiment of the difference it could make. He was glad to see that Tol circled out well wide of the place where Nightlife had entered the woods.

In his battered and frazzled old straw hat that no longer by its shape distinguished front from back, and his increasingly disheveled clothes now soaked with sweat, Tol reminded Sam of a germinating seed, as though he might at any moment burst out of his deteriorating rind of woven fabric and become a tree. He had about him already something of the staunchness and the surprising sizableness of a tree. He was like a tree walking. Over the difficult terrain of that day he had taken the footing as it came, uphill or down, sidling or flat, brushy or open, trudging forward as implacably as a draft horse at work, as concentrated in his way as Nightlife in his.

The others also were coming now, hurrying to catch up, Walter Cotman and the Hardys positioning themselves in relation to Tol as before, Put Woolfork falling back into his accustomed place at the rear.

Their little delay at the cistern had cost them; now, for the first time since the beginning, they did not have Nightlife in sight and did not know in which direction he had gone. Once they were in the woods, they circled back toward the point of his entry in order to cross his track. They took their time, watching and being careful.

In a little while Walter Cotman said quietly, "Here he went."

And now they arranged themselves according to the known reference of Nightlife's track, which curved around a slue and then on out of the woods into another grass field where, at last, they had him in sight again.

From the barn where they drank, Nightlife had not gone back to the river, but slanted across the bottom generally in the direction of the mouth of Willow Run. He went on as before, straying around impassable obstacles, avoiding places where there might be people. For Tol and the others, following him had ceased to seem unusual. In the heat and the difficulty of their constant effort to keep just within sight of their strange neighbor—who had become at once their fear, their quarry, and their leader—they had ceased even to wonder what end they were moving toward. This wild pursuit that at first had seemed an interruption of their work had become their work. Now they could hardly imagine what they would be doing if they were home.

At the edge of a tobacco patch, they came upon two rows of tomatoes. Going by, they each picked two or three ripe ones. Tom Hardy picked a half-rotten one and aimed a perfect throw at the back of his brother's head. If the tomato had been anything harder, it would have knocked Braymer down. Braymer returned the fire with two tomatoes, one of which, aimed at Tom's head, caused him to duck, the second knocking off his hat. This exchange occurred in perfect good humor and in absolute silence.

Tol, who had a large tomato in each hand, whispered, "Boys! Boys! Boys!" and kept walking.

Tom made as if to throw a tomato at Tol's back, grinned at his brother, and followed Tol, eating the tomato.

Nightlife reached the river again just a little downstream from the mouth of Willow Run. He kicked aside a few little pieces of driftwood and made himself a place to sit down and then he sat down, leaning his back against a large sycamore. There were several big trees there, water maples and sycamores and cottonwoods, making the shade deep.

A good breeze, the first they had felt all day, was coming up the river. They would have been comfortable, waiting there, except that they were thirsty again, and even if they had wanted to drink out of the river in dog days, they could not have gone down the bank now without putting themselves too much into view.

And so they just stopped when Nightlife stopped, and stood still, only taking their hats off to let the breeze cool their heads. After they had been there, unmoving, a little while, the stillness of the place sealed itself over them. Even the little wind ripples on the water seemed to grow attentive and still.

And that was when they heard Put Woolfork squall. It was really not much of a squall, just the single abrupt syllable, "Wa!"—a statement that Put would not be allowed to forget for the rest of his life. It might have been merely the startled, despairing outcry of some unfortunate animal.

But Tol knew what it was, and he thought, "Boys!"

If Nightlife had heard, he gave no sign. He did not move. Tol looked then to see which of his young companions was missing, and found that none was. They were all looking at him.

He started back toward the place the squall had come from. Seeing that all four of the others had started back with him, he stopped; he motioned to Sam to stay and keep an eye on Nightlife, and then went on, Walter and the Hardys moving quietly along with him.

Presently they saw, standing at the foot of a tall cottonwood, Burley Coulter with three days' whiskers and holding an unlit lantern, grinning at Put Woolfork, who was fussing at him in a whisper.

"It ain't a damn bit funny," Put was saying. "You just done it because it was me. I'd like to see you try it on Walter Cotman."

Burley simply continued to grin. And then when he saw Tol and Walter and the Hardys coming up, he shifted his grin to them.

For a few seconds nobody said anything, and then Tol said, "I knowed it was a boy. I just didn't know which boy it was."

Burley was twenty-one that year, old enough to take

the word *boy* either as a judgment or as a joke. Tol offered it as both, and Burley received it with his grin unaltered.

"Howdy, Burley," Walter Cotman said. "Has Put treed a squirrel?"

Burley told what there was to tell. He had been in a patch of elderberries at the edge of the riverbank trees, just ready to step into the shade to cool off and maybe take a swim in the river, when he saw Nightlife coming along with the gun; Burley recognized it as Tol's Old Fetcher. From Nightlife's possession of the gun, and from the look of him, Burley knew that something was out of fix. He kept still. Presently he saw Tol and Sam and Walter and the Hardy brothers, who obviously were following Nightlife. And then, coming way behind, he saw Put. When Tol and the others stopped, Put, who could not see Nightlife, stepped behind the big cottonwood and began to peep around it. He was so given over to his curiosity that Burley could not resist the temptation to creep up behind him and poke him in the back with a stick. Thereupon, expecting to die, Put had uttered the aforementioned famous exclamation.

The circumstances did not permit laughter, but even Tol smiled.

And Put said, "Slip up on a fellow that way! It's about what you'd expect."

"If you expected it, what did you holler for?" Burley said.

Burley was a wild young man. As the others knew,

Put was an eager carrier of tales about Burley; they knew that Burley knew it, and knew that Put knew that Burley knew it.

"Well, what are *you* doing here?" Walter asked Burley.

"I've got a young dog disappeared over in here somewhere. Running a fox, I reckon."

"How come you're hunting this time of year?"

"I ain't hunting. *He's* hunting. I'm hunting *him*. You all got anything to eat? I had a few biscuits but they're long gone."

"No. We ain't got a crumb. How long you been gone?"

Burley grinned, not much wanting to say, but finally saying, "Since night before last. What you boys doing?"

They told him.

Put, whose sense of grievance had been growing, said, "It's done already chore time. I got to go home."

"Don't go, Put," Tol said. He knew that was what Put wanted him to say, but he said it anyhow. "It ain't no use in going."

"Well," Put said sadly, "I ain't got no business here."

Having thus expressed his dissatisfaction with them all, Put headed home.

And so, while following Nightlife to keep from losing him somewhere ahead of them, they had lost Put

Woolfork behind them. And Tol was sorry, for he had not meant to lose anybody. He knew Put exactly for what he was. And yet in some way that Tol could not have explained, now that Put had gone off offended, they needed him. Or anyhow Tol did.

"He ain't going home yet," Walter said. "Not till his women have had time to get the milking done."

"Well," Tol said, "he don't mean no harm."

"Nor no good neither."

"Well, but no harm."

Tol was not sure there was no harm in Put—he was at least a gossip and probably a troublemaker—but he did not want to say so, and he did not want Walter to say so. It was a time of day when you could be sorrowful if you were not at home. Tol felt himself pressed out again onto that verge that Nightlife was walking. The conviction welled up in him that Put was better with them than he was alone—even allowing for the trouble that attended him, or that he brought, when he was with them.

"How about you boys?" he asked. "You all have got chores, too."

"Well, how about you?" Braymer Hardy said.

"I ain't got much. Miss Minnie can do what I've got."

"Well, our wives can do ours," Braymer said.

"How about Josie?" Tol said to Tom Hardy, who was the one most recently married. "Can she milk?"

"Why, I reckon!" Braymer said. "She's a better hand than Tom."

"Walter," Tom said, "can you do like Put and leave your chores for your wife?"

"Why, sure," Walter said.

Tol—who had not ceased to watch Sam Hanks, who had not ceased to watch Nightlife—now saw Sam motion to them to come on.

"Come on, boys," Tol said.

"Burley," Walter Cotman said, "you just as well go with us."

"I reckon I just as well," Burley said.

And so he came along.

*F*rom the mouth of Willow Run, where the river curved in close to the hill again, Nightlife led them back up along the wooded bluffs. Now they left the river valley and walked upstream along the westward slope of the valley of Willow Run. Once he was well up into the woods, Nightlife followed the level contour of the slope out around the points and in and out of the hollows, as he had done before, and they followed him.

In one hollow a tiny stream of water flowed, and Nightlife followed it straight up the slope to where a spring issued from a cleft in a ledge of rock. They watched him kneel and drink, and waited while he sat down to rest.

Waiting, they looked at one another and grinned. They were again suffering from thirst, and again Night-life took his time.

When finally he rose and went on and disappeared in the foliage, Tol motioned to Burley to go and drink. There was room for only one to drink at a time, and Tol did not want as much commotion and delay as there had been at the barn.

They watched as Burley knelt and drank and went on, and then one by one Tol waved the others forward: Walter, and then the two Hardys, and then Sam.

When Sam had finished, Tol drank and followed after the others, leaving the woods quiet again around the spring.

They would be in the woods now for a long time, for the west slope of the valley was poor land, most of which had been cut over at one time or another but not plowed. They were passing through some stands of large trees, mostly hickory and oak, and it was pretty walking, though too steep to be comfortable. Going along behind the others, Tol thought that if he were not hungry and did not have Nightlife to worry about, he would be having a pretty good time. And then he thought that he was having a pretty good time anyhow.

The evening shade had come to that side of the valley by the time Tol caught up with the others. It was cooling off a little. They would have been grateful for some supper—they were all thinking of things they would like to eat—but they were enjoying the cool. A little breeze had begun drifting down the slope, drying the sweat from their faces.

The light now lost its strength and heat as if detached from its source. Stray glows and luminescences floated among the trees. Sometimes they would hear a wood thrush sing, a flute suddenly trilled and then fading, somewhere beyond or behind. And before all the daylight was gone, there was a moon.

While Tol still had enough light to see them all, he gathered them to him. "We can't all stay close enough to see him after dark," he said. "So let Burley follow Nightlife, and we'll follow Burley. With that moon, we ought to be able to stay together pretty good."

And that was what they did.

After it got dark, Nightlife wandered a little more than he had earlier; he went a little slower and stopped more often. But he went on and on, Burley followed him, and they followed Burley. They kept always alert, for if Burley lost sight of Nightlife or they lost sight of Burley, anything could happen. Or so they felt. They felt that they could not afford to risk confusion. They certainly did not want to become disoriented and blunder into Nightlife and Old Fetcher in the dark. Enough moonlight filtered down through the foliage to give vigilance an edge over confusion, but barely enough. The light filled

the woods with shadows, and at times the very effort of
sight seemed to call forth phantoms and apparitions,
motions where nothing moved. They lost all sense of
where they were except in relation to one another. They
forgot their tiredness and their hunger. They would have
been thirsty again if they had thought of it, but they
had forgotten thirst. They seemed to have become en-
larged out of their bodies into sight itself and the effort
of sight, and they walked owl-eyed among the confusions
of things and the shadows of things.

They knew only what they saw, and they saw only
shadows within a shadow. Nightlife led them through a
maze that did not exist before he led them through it.
They went in silence, for the dew had softened the dry
leaves underfoot, and still they walked with care. Now
and again, when they passed above a house, dogs would
bark. Now and again, way off, they would hear an owl.
Once, coming suddenly to the edge of an open field, they
seemed to plunge headlong out of the dark into the moon-
flooded sky.

The moon shone way into the night. And then,
unexpectedly, for they had not seen the sky in a while,
clouds covered the moon, and it was suddenly so dark
that they could not see to the ends of their own arms;
when they held their hands up before their faces and
wiggled their fingers, they could not see them. It was,
Walter Cotman told Elton Penn, who told me, "as black
as a coker's ass, and all at once."

They stopped and waited, for that was all they could do. They knew that somewhere in the dark ahead of them Burley was trying out the problem of following Nightlife by sound, or of getting close enough to him to know where he was without touching him. And so they waited.

They waited a long time, and saw nothing at all. They heard anonymous, inexplicable stirrings here and there. They heard a dog bark, way off—not at them this time. They heard a small owl trill sweetly and another answer from farther away. And that was all.

They were beginning to think of sitting down when they saw a dim yellow light suddenly bloom out of a hollow not far behind them. They turned and eased back toward it. When they got close enough, they recognized Burley. He had lit his lantern. They gathered around him.

"He never stopped," Burley said. "He kept right on going."

"Course he went on!" Walter said. "A man that can't see in the daytime, what does it matter to him if he can't see in the dark?"

"I stayed with him for a while," Burley said. "I was close enough to him that I could hear him walking, I thought. And then I got to where I couldn't tell what I was hearing. I was starting to hear things, and I couldn't tell if they was actually things or not. I got scared I'd walk smack into him, so I held back. And then I lost him. He either stopped or went on, I don't know which."

"Well, we don't want that light, do we?" Tol said.

"He's too far to see it where he is," Burley said, "I think, unless he followed me back." He grinned at Walter Cotman.

The lantern, turned low, sat on the ground at their feet. It showed them their faces, and cast their shadows out around them like the spokes of a wheel.

They fell silent now, for the knowledge of their failure had suddenly come over them. The potency of Tol's old shotgun entered their thoughts again. They knew that at any time, from somewhere out in the dark, they might hear its one short and final exclamation. And only then would they know where to go.

"Well," Tol Proudfoot said, after a time that seemed longer than it was, "I reckon we've lost him."

"I reckon if he's lost, he ain't by hisself," Tom Hardy said. "Do you know where we are?"

"I know within three or four miles, I reckon," Tol said.

"Do you know, Burley?"

"Right here," Burley said.

They were speaking almost in whispers.

"What're we going to do, then?" Walter Cotman said. "Stand here till sunup, with that lantern lighting us up for him to shoot at?"

"That lantern ain't going to burn till sunup," Burley said, "unless one of you all brought some coal oil."

"We could build us a little fire, I reckon," Braymer said.

Tol knew then that they were going to build a fire. He already objected to the lantern—or the caution in him objected to it. But after the darkness, it was a comfort and a pleasure. That they would build a fire he knew because he knew he could not bring himself to stop them from building it.

He was nonetheless relieved to hear Walter Cotman say, "We're too close to him here to build any fire."

"Well," Burley said, "we could drop down through this hollow till we're out of the woods. He'll stay in the woods, won't he? That's his pattern."

They made their way slowly down the rocky bed of the stream. They came to a water gap in a rock fence, and crossed into what they knew to be a pasture, for now they saw cattle tracks and smelled cattle, and the foliage had been browsed to the height of a man. There were trees still along the hollow, but here there would be grass fields out on the slopes on either side.

Burley led them up out of the streambed onto a little bench. By the light of the lantern or by feel they gathered up kindling and bigger wood for a fire. They helped the kindling with a tiny splatter of oil from the lantern, and soon they had a small fire going. Burley raised the globe and blew out the lantern flame. The fire cheered them; it forced back the dark and the damp of the night a little, and they were glad to sit down beside it. They were tired, and the fire made them a resting place.

And yet sitting there in the room of light it made was a fearfully simple, almost a brutal, act of faith. It made them visible to all the distances around them, and made those distances invisible to them. All they could hope was that if Nightlife saw the light of their fire, he would come into it and not shoot into it. They did not *think* he would see it, but the chance that he might shaped that odd little hope in them, and it kept them silent for a while, glowing, all of them, in the firelight.

Finally Walter Cotman said quietly, "It'll rain tomorrow."

"I'd say so," Tol said.

"Well, we need a rain."

"Yes, we do. If it don't come too hard."

"It could come hard. It's been mighty hot."

"We need one of them good old dizz-dozzlers," Braymer Hardy said. "This time of year, it would be money in the bank."

"A good rain now surely would ruin them little cabbages of mine," Tol said.

"Why?"

"It would make big ones out of 'em."

What they had said had not made so welcome an effect on the silence around them as their fire had made on the darkness. They let the silence come back. The fire eased them, and they thought of their tobacco. Walter and Burley made cigarettes; Sam and Tol filled and lit cob pipes; the others took chews.

After a while Walter said in the same quiet voice as before, "Tom, you reckon Josie'll still be at your house when you get home?"

"It ain't every newly married man that you find wandering about the woods of a night," Tol said.

"Pore thing," Braymer said, "it's just a blessing she don't care nothing about him, or this sort of doings would break her heart."

Except for Tom's, every face around the fire remained solemn. Tom grinned.

Tol said, "You take a young fellow like that, now, ugly and mean and nothing to offer but beans and hard work, and he fools a nice, smart, pretty girl into marrying him—you'd think he wouldn't leave home, day nor night."

"It's a shame," Walter said. "The women are all talking about it."

"I growed my crop close to the house, the first year I got married," Braymer said, "didn't you, Uncle Tol?"

"Yessir, I did," Tol said.

"Tom," Walter said, "when you get up of a morning and you see these little specks floating on top of your coffee and you try to blow them off and they don't blow off, that's because they ain't there."

And then, way off, on their side of the valley but

in a place they had not yet come to, they heard a hound's voice open the darkness like a flare.

They hushed to listen.

The hound puzzled for several minutes over the scent he had announced, as if he were cold-trailing, perhaps, or going in the wrong direction. And then his cries rose full and confident.

"Is that your dog, Burley?" Sam Hanks asked.

"It's him," Burley said.

"Well, that ain't no fox he's running now."

"No. He's running a coon now."

Tol said, "He's a sweet-mouthed dog, ain't he?"

They listened. Presently the cries became more urgent. The coon had treed.

"That was quick," Sam said.

"Probably a sow with young ones," Burley said.

The hound's voice now seemed to fill the world with longing. The voice seemed to speak for the world. It spoke for Nightlife. It spoke for them all.

It seemed to them also to be an outrageous breach of propriety—so close and, in the face of their difficulty, so insistent on the normal order of things. The hound was Burley's, and the others kept quiet for fear that Burley was going to say, in spite of Nightlife's despair somewhere nearby in the dark, "Well, I reckon we ought to go see if a coon is what it is." Burley himself kept quiet for fear that one of the others might say it in deference

to him. And so for a long time nobody but the hound
said anything.

Without warning, a hectoring, humorous voice
came out of the nearby dark: "Well, by God, if you
fellows is hunting, why don't you go to your dog?"

The voice lifted them to varying heights above their
resting places before they recognized it and let themselves
back down again. Lester Proudfoot stepped into the firelight, holding his lantern up as if he had found what he
was looking for.

"We ain't hunting," Burley said. "We're just sitting here improving."

"I don't reckon you brought anything to eat," Tom
Hardy said. "Or drink."

"Naw, nor nothing to sleep with neither. What in
the hell are *you* doing, running around in the woods of
a night? Something got wrong with young women since
my day? Tol, how you making it?"

Lester bore all the distinguishing marks of a Proudfoot. He was Tol's first cousin, and he looked like Tol,
though he was not as big. He possessed to the full the
Proudfoot gregariousness, always ready to do anything
that could be done in company. Lester would talk to
anybody anywhere, under any circumstances, at any time,
at any length. A hunter himself, he had been awakened

by the hound and then, looking out his kitchen window, had seen the fire up on the hillside.

Tol told him why they were there.

"And Nightlife's up yonder in the woods somewhere with a gun?" Lester said.

"I reckon. Sit down, Les."

Lester sat down. He extinguished his lantern. "And you boys is waiting here either for him to see this fire and come to it, or take a shot at one of you all."

"Or shoot hisself," Walter Cotman said. "Or wander on from hell to breakfast, the way he's been doing."

"He's done already wandered around equal to Moses," Tom Hardy said.

"He's wandered around equal to old Daniel Boone hisself," Braymer said.

"Well, I hope he discovers Kentucky pretty soon and settles down," Walter said.

"What the matter with him is he's a Hample," Lester said. "Ain't that his chief difficulty? He don't fit the hole that was bored for him."

"Les," Tol said, "tell about that time Nightlife's granddaddy swore off drinking."

"Uncle Norey," Lester said. "Uncle Norey got to where he would always get drunk and down before the crop was made, and leave the hardest part for Aunt Nancy and the children. Aunt Nancy told him he'd have to stop that, and he did, he swore off. And then when they finally got the crop made and ready for the market, Uncle

Norey said, 'Here I've put in a whole crop year from Genesis to Revelation, and nare a drop of liquor has defiled my lips. Hand me that jug!' "

After Lester's noisy entrance among them, their conversation had been quiet. Now they laughed as quietly as they had spoken. And then, except for the hound still clamoring at the tree, the quiet restored itself.

For some time, where they were, it was silent altogether.

And then Tom Hardy said, "A man would think of killing hisself, he ain't at hisself, surely."

"He's at hisself, all right," Tol said. "He ain't nowhere *but* at hisself. Look at old Nightlife just rambling on, not looking right nor left, going like he knows where, and he don't know."

"The way he is now," Walter said, "he just as well stayed home or stayed asleep. Or never been born. He don't know where he is."

"Don't matter where he is," Tol said. "He's just wandering around inside hisself, looking for the way out. In there where he is, it's dark sure enough."

"Well, here we are. Or there we were. Right there with him."

"And what did we do? Or what could we? For he ain't just wandering around inside hisself; he's wandering around out of reach—by about the range of that old gun."

"You got to live whether you want to or not," Tom Hardy said.

Tol said, "Boy, I think you've got to want to." He said nothing for a long time then, and then he said, "You've got to *like* to live in this world. You can't just mortal it out from one day to the next for three score years and ten."

They were quiet again for a while, and then Lester stood up and relit his lantern. He said, "I reckon being as that keen-eyed fellow's up there with Tol's gun, I won't bother about your dog now, Burley. I'll slip up there after daylight and bring him down to the house. You get him when you can."

"I'd be much obliged," Burley said.

Lester stepped out of the firelight then. For a few seconds they heard his footsteps descending the slope, and then it was quiet. They could hear the hound, and that was all.

When Lester had gone, they began to feel their weariness. One by one they lay down beside the fire and slept.

"Couldn't you stay awake? Couldn't you stay awake?"

Gray daylight had come. The fire had burned down to white ash. Now, though the hound was exactly where he had been before, his voice sounded farther away and smaller. But what had wakened them was Nightlife standing over them, one foot in the ashes. He was holding the gun, but not threatening them with it. It dangled from his hand as unregarded as if it had been the bail of an empty bucket.

"Couldn't you stay awake?"

The lenses of his glasses apparently as opaque as bark, he was looking right at them and not seeing them. They were frightened, astonished, tickled at their own and one another's fright and astonishment, and most of all ashamed.

"Sit down, Nightlife," Tol said. "Sit down, old bud. We'll go home pretty soon and get some breakfast."

"You think there ain't no breakfast here?" Nightlife said. "Where the hell you think breakfast is at? I've got breakfast right here."

His voice had grown louder, and now he raised the gun and gestured with it in a way that caused them to make various motions backward. "Couldn't you stay awake?" he said.

"Well, we thought if you shot yourself it would wake us up," said Walter Cotman.

Nightlife went on then. He stepped out of the circle of men around the dead fire, and started back up into the woods. They lay there with their heads raised and watched him go.

"Shoo!" Tom Hardy said quietly. It seemed to them all that they now began to breathe again.

Tol grunted, getting himself to his feet. "If he hadn't found us," he said, "I don't reckon we ever would have found him."

The others got up slowly and followed—"three meals in arrears by then," Sam Hanks would say years later, "and we were feeling it, I can tell you."

It was not long before it seemed to them that they had never stopped. They went on as before. Even their hunger and thirst were familiar. They came to another spring and drank, and then they were only hungry.

*T*hey were going upstream through the woods on the westward side of Willow Run valley, which was the eastward side of Cotman Ridge, the westward side of which they had gone down the morning before. They were approaching Tol Proudfoot's place from the direction opposite to that of their departure.

When Nightlife stopped again, Tol dropped back a little and beckoned Sam to him.

"Looks like we'll be pretty close to home again before long," he said.

"Maybe he'll circle right back to there," Sam said. "You reckon?"

"Maybe so. If he don't, maybe we can at least get a bite to eat as we go by. If you don't mind, would you just cut straight across to my house and ask Miss Minnie would she kindly see if she can't scrape us up a little something to eat?"

"Why, sure," Sam said. "Looks like that Nightlife would get hungry sooner or later hisself. Don't you reckon a good meal mightn't get him unfittified?"

"It might," Tol said. "There's a world of sanity in a little meat and gravy. It sho would help me."

The women, of course, had anticipated this hunger. When Sam stepped into Miss Minnie's kitchen, Thelma Cotman and the two Josie Hardys, Josie Braymer and Josie Tom, were frying chicken and baking biscuits and making gravy and slicing tomatoes and boiling beans and potatoes. Even old Mrs. Hample, Nightlife's mother, was there. Miss Minnie had sent for her, and she had walked up not long after daylight, worried and needing company. She was making a kind of dutiful effort to help the other women, but was so distracted and full of hesitations that she was only getting in their way, moving about more aimlessly than not, wringing her hands beneath her apron and trying to disguise her repeated glances out the windows and the door. "I just don't know what's got into that boy's head," she kept saying. "I just wisht I knowed."

The smell in the kitchen was almost too much for Sam Hanks. "I thought I was going to faint," he said. "I had to sit down and hold onto the table."

But he delivered his message: one way or another,

sooner or later, they would be there to eat. They would need a lot. They were hungry.

"I should think so," Miss Minnie said. "Poor Thacker Hample!"

"Poor Thacker Hample!" Sam said. "Good God!"

To appease him and to comfort him on his walk back into the woods, she gave him two chicken legs and three biscuits, which in pure kindness Sam ate in a hurry, so as not to torment Tol and the others by the sight.

*I*t was not a true circle that Nightlife had traveled in. He had been governed too much both by the lay of the land and by his craziness for his course to have assumed any sort of regular shape. Nevertheless, it was clear by midmorning that he was headed back toward their starting place. He came up out of the woods and began picking his way across the pastures and hayfields and around the tobacco and corn patches of the ridgetop, and he was tending generally in the direction of Tol Proudfoot's place.

For some time they had been hearing thunder in the distance, and every leaf in the woods had held still. When they came out of the woods onto the high and open ground, they could see under the general overcast a dark cloud sharply outlined above the horizon in the southwest. And the thunder was louder. They could hear it rumbling and stuttering. It had about it the quality of preoccupation, as if the Power inhabiting the cloud was as yet too intent upon his preparations to concern himself much with what he was going to do.

Keeping Nightlife in sight was no longer a problem now that they were on the open ridge. He went his way as before, looking neither left nor right, as if he were the only human being left on earth. Tol and the others maintained their distance from him, safely out of gun range, close enough to see him. When they got to the top of the ridge and could look down and see Tol's house and outbuildings, Tol beckoned to Sam and Burley and Walter.

"Boys, work your way around on the right now. Stay between him and the house. *Don't* let him go to the house. Sam, you go tell the women to lock the doors."

So now their configuration changed. Tol and the Hardys followed Nightlife as before, but Walter and Burley and Sam walked almost even with him, well out to his right. And now the sky lowered and darkened until it seemed to enclose them all in a breathless and rapidly shrinking room.

The road across from Tol's place was bordered by a rock fence. Because they were approaching at an angle to the road, the three who were walking to Nightlife's right got to the fence before he did, and crossed it and stepped down the bank into the road. Nightlife then approached the fence and started to cross.

And that was the last that Tol and the Hardys saw

of him before the storm hit. It fell upon them all of a
sudden—lightning and thunder and wind and hard rain
all at once. Tom and Braymer started running and also
disappeared from sight. The rain fell hard, so nearly a
solid spout that, Burley said, "a fish could have swum
up it." When the big drops struck and splashed, the
wind seized the spray and sped it along in sheets.

Tol went down the slope to the rock fence, clambered over it, fell, and slid down the bank into the road.
He glimpsed the opening of the driveway, and went in
under the greater darkness of the yard trees. By then he,
too, was running.

The shop was the first outbuilding reachable from
the road. And now Tol could see that the door of the
shop was open, and he knew the others had gone inside.
He was not fast on his feet, but he passed one other man
who, he realized only after he had gone by, was walking,
and carrying a gun.

"No, boys!" he called into the shop as he ran.
"Wait! Come out!"

He stumbled into the dark interior of the shop only
a step or two ahead of Nightlife, who stopped as soon as
he got inside the door.

When Nightlife stepped through the door behind
Tol, and took his stand just inside, cradling the gun in
his hands as if expecting a covey of quail to flush at any

second, that put an end to the little breathless laughter that had started among the others because of their wild run through the storm and their escape into shelter at last.

They hushed and stood still in their sopping clothes. Sam Hanks then quietly sat down on a nail keg in front of the forge. Now that they looked at Nightlife face to face, after all he had caused them to do and to think, they were struck by how ordinary he looked. He looked like his same old self—except that, looking straight at them, he appeared not to see them, or to be looking through them at whatever was behind them.

"Brethren," he said, "let us stand and sing." And he began, alone at first, to sing "The Unclouded Day."

Staggeringly, the others began to join in. And here it was discovered that Sam Hanks, who was the only one sitting down, had not stood up. He had instead managed to find a dry match and had lit his pipe.

"Sam," Tom Hardy said to him in a whisper, "ain't you going to sing?"

"*Naw*sir!" Sam said out loud. "I ain't a-going to sing just because the likes of him tells me to."

"Well, he's liable to shoot you."

"Well, he'll just have to do it then, because I ain't going to sing." And Sam expelled several small complacent puffs of smoke, looking out past Nightlife into the rain.

But the others sang, and sang pretty well, too, Burley's and Tol's strong voices carrying the others:

> O the land of cloudless day,
> O the land of an unclouded day;
> O they tell me of a home where no storm clouds rise,
> O they tell me of an unclouded day.

They lifted the fine old song up against the rattle of hard rain on the roof and up over the roof and out into the gray, raining light—as if in them the neighborhood sang, even under threat, its love for itself and its grief for itself, greater than the terms of this world allow. By the time they got to the second verse, the onsetting force of the storm having abated, Miss Minnie and Thelma and the two Josies and old Mrs. Hample could hear them all the way to the kitchen, and I can hear them now:

> O they tell me of a home where my friends have gone,
> O they tell me of a land far away,
> Where the tree of life in eternal bloom
> Sheds its fragrance thro' the unclouded day.

When they finished the hymn, Nightlife began his sermon—the one, as they supposed, that he had prepared for the revival service of the night before last. His text was Matthew 18:12, which he knew by heart:

How think ye? if a man have an hundred sheep,
and one of them be gone astray, doth he not
leave the ninety and nine, and goeth into the
mountains, and seeketh that which is gone
astray?

Though Christ, in speaking this parable, asked his hearers
to think of the shepherd, Nightlife understood it entirely
from the viewpoint of the lost sheep, who could imagine
fully the condition of being lost and even the hope of
rescue, but could not imagine rescue itself.

"Oh, it's a dark place, my brethren," Nightlife said.
"It's a dark place where the lost sheep tries to find his
way, and can't. The slopes is steep and the footing hard.
The ground is rough and stumbly and dark, and over-
growed with bushes and briars, a hilly and a hollery place.
And the shepherd comes a-looking and a-calling to his
lost sheep, and the sheep knows the shepherd's voice and
he wants to go to it, but he can't find the path, and he
can't make it."

The others knew that Nightlife knew what he was
talking about. They knew he was telling what it was to
be him. And they were moved.

Long afterward, Elton Penn asked Walter Cotman,
"Did what he said make sense? I mean, did you feel for
him?"

"Me?" Walter said. "*Course* I felt for him! The son
of a bitch could preach!"

They were moved. Even Sam Hanks was moved. But they also began to be amused—begging sympathy's pardon—because Miss Minnie's old setting hen had returned from wherever she had been to breakfast, only to find Nightlife standing and preaching right in front of her nest. The hen began to walk back and forth at Nightlife's feet, crying out with rapidly increasing hysteria, "My children! My children! What will become of my children?" Now and again, she squatted and opened her wings as if to fly up to her nest, and then changed her mind.

At last she crouched almost directly in front of Nightlife, and with a leap, a desperate, panic-stricken, determined outcry, and a great flapping of wings, she launched herself upward.

But she had miscalculated Nightlife's height; he continued to rise up in front of her long past the point at which she had expected him to stop. She got up a little above breast height, and then either lost her nerve or decided to stop and reconsider. She hung there, flapping and squawking, right in Nightlife's face, and Nightlife struck her an open-handed blow that Walter Cotman said would have given second thoughts to a mule.

After Nightlife hit the hen, Walter told Elton, she hung suspended in the air for many seconds, whirling like a pinwheel and shedding feathers around her in spirals.

———

*A*nd that was all it took. By the time the hen hit the ground, still squawking, a change had come over Nightlife. He looked around like a man just awakened, and it was plain to the others that he saw that they were there with him and that he knew them. It looked to them as though the very lenses of his glasses were clarified by intelligence. He leaned the shotgun against the bench, and stood free of it.

Tol then stepped up beside Nightlife and picked up the gun. He said, "Nightlife, honey, I want you to see my gun. My daddy had it before me. It's an old one."

He opened the breech, removed the shell, and put the shell into his pocket. He snapped the breech shut again and handed the gun to Nightlife, who took it and looked it over.

"It looks like a right good old gun, Tol," Nightlife said, and he handed it back.

They heard the dinner bell then, for Miss Minnie, feeling that she should do something, and not knowing what else to do, had sent Josie Tom out to ring it.

"Boys," Tol said, "I believe Old Marster and the good women have kept us in mind. Let's go eat!"

"*O*h, that was a meal that was a joy to set on the table!" Miss Minnie said.

She and her nephew, Sam Hanks, had been telling Granny and me the story of Nightlife's spell and his long ramble through the woods. It had taken most of the afternoon. Miss Minnie's account of all they had to eat and of all they ate had been a small epic in itself.

It was a story I never forgot, and as time went on I would pick up bits of it from Braymer Hardy, from Walter Cotman by way of Elton Penn, and from others. But Miss Minnie, I think, understood it better than anybody. She had taught at least four of those young men at the Goforth school: Nightlife, Burley Coulter, and the two Hardys. And she and Tol had been neighbors to them all. She knew pretty exactly by what precarious interplay of effort and grace the neighborhood had lived.

"Poor old Thacker Hample," she said. "They kept him alive that time, anyhow. They and the Good Lord."

"And that old hen," Sam Hanks said.

"Yes, that old hen," Miss Minnie said.

She mused a while, rocking in her chair. Finally she said, "And don't you know that old hen survived it all. She hatched fourteen chicks and raised them, every one!"